VICTIM 69

RASOOL DARWEESH
A novelist, critic and translator. The author of:
The Sin of the Cellar (2013)
Dilmunia (2016)
The Black Stone (2017)
Christ of the East (Drama) (2019)
The Soul of the King (2021)
Children of the Rainbow (2021)
Booker at Stake (Criticism) (2021)
I Don't Love You (Translated Poems) (2022)
Richness of Poverty (2023)
De Baren (2023)
The Book of Identities (Criticism) (2023)
Victim 69 (Arabic Edition) (2023)

HASAN MARHAMAH
The translator/author of:
Voices I: An Annotated Anthology of Contemporary Bahraini Poetry (2009)
Voices II: Contemporary Bahraini Short Stories (2014)
Voices: An Anthology Contemporary Bahraini Poetry (2015)
The Bright Field: The Poetry of Ronald Stuart Thomas (in Arabic) (2015)
A Glossary of Literary & Critical Terms (2019)
Contemporary Literary & Critical Schools (in Arabic) (2021)

VICTIM 69

Rasool Darweesh

Translated by Hasan Marhamah

Copyright © 2024 Rasool Darweesh

The moral right of the author has been asserted.

Apart from any fair dealing for the purposes of research or private study, or criticism or review, as permitted under the Copyright, Designs and Patents Act 1988, this publication may only be reproduced, stored or transmitted, in any form or by any means, with the prior permission in writing of the publishers, or in the case of reprographic reproduction in accordance with the terms of licences issued by the Copyright Licensing Agency. Enquiries concerning reproduction outside those terms should be sent to the publishers.

This is a work of fiction. Names, characters, businesses, places, events and incidents are either the products of the author's imagination or used in a fictitious manner. Any resemblance to actual persons, living or dead, or actual events is purely coincidental.

Troubador Publishing Ltd
Unit E2 Airfield Business Park,
Harrison Road, Market Harborough,
Leicestershire LE16 7UL
Tel: 0116 279 2299
Email: books@troubador.co.uk
Web: www.troubador.co.uk

ISBN 978-1-80514-489-2

British Library Cataloguing in Publication Data.
A catalogue record for this book is available from the British Library.

Printed and bound in Great Britain by 4edge Limited
Typeset in 11pt Minion Pro by Troubador Publishing Ltd, Leicester, UK

To Khawla,
who still lives the pain of parting,
in *Dilmunia*.

Foreword

A novelist writes in a language inherited from his predecessors and puts his ideas in context, expressing his style in a state of unconsciousness. This unconsciousness shocks the writer himself after dissociating himself from his text. He would not know if he wrote that piece or vice versa! This leaves the text throbbing with life. I ended up writing *Victim 69* in that same vein.

Rasool Darweesh

A List of Characters and Names in Alphabetical Order

Abdul Rahman Bin Isa: Advisor at the University of Al Qassim and Warsaw's third husband by *misyaar* marriage and the father of Isa.

Abdul Wahab: An Egyptian singer and composer.

Aboudi: Short for Abdullah.

Abu Adel: Warsaw's stepfather.

Abu Humood: Um Humood's husband.

Abu Musa: Warsaw's first husband.

Adil Emam: An Egyptian comic actor.

A'aedh: Warsaw's second husband.

Al Mutanabi: An Arab poet who lived during the Abbasid Caliphate (915–965).

Baha: The Asian driver.

Dr. Sa'ad: The critic and narrator.

Fairuz: A Lebanese female singer.

George Qardahi: A Lebanese TV presenter.

Hamdan: Warsaw's uncle.

Harayeb: Um Humood's first name.

Hessa: Warsaw's mother.

Ibn Baz: Islamic scholar and Grand Mufti of Saudi Arabia.

Isa: Warsaw's son.

Jaza'a: Um Rabi'a's first name.

Musa: Warsaw's son from first husband.

Najib Mahfudh: An Egyptian novelist and Noble Prize winner.

Swar: Warsaw's daughter from first husband.

Um Humood: The midwife.

Um Isa: Warsaw.

Um Kulthum: An Egyptian female singer.

Um Rabi'a: The wet nurse.

Warda: An Algerian female singer.

Warsaw: The protagonist and narrator.

A List of Cities and Towns in Alphabetical Order

Al Madina: A city in the west of Saudi Arabia.

Al Qassim: A province in the north of Saudi Arabia.

Buraydah: A city in the province of Al Qassim in Saudi Arabia.

Hael: A city in the north of Saudi Arabia.

Hafre Al Batten: A city in the Eastern Province in Saudi Arabia.

Hijrat Aljabhan: A village in the north of Saudi Arabia.

Jabal Auhud: A mountain in Yemen.

Manama: The capital of Bahrain.

Rafhaa: A city in the north of Saudi Arabia.

Riyadh: The capital of Saudi Arabia.

Shammar: A tribe living in Hael in Saudi Arabia and other Arabian states.

A List of Arabic/Local Terms and Phrases in Alphabetical Order

Al Eddah: Waiting period required for a divorcee.

Al Haya: Religious supervisory committee.

Bint: Daughter of.

Daq/Daqqa: Tattoo.

Day of Judgement: The day when all human beings will be judged by Allah.

Derrida: Beautiful.

Haijna: A local Bedouin song.

Halal: Allowed according to Islamic religion.

Haraam: Prohibited or not allowed according to Islamic religion.

Hurma: A woman.

In Shaa'allah: God willing.

Iqal: Head tie for men.

Jelf: Filth, an epithet used for men.

Kabsat Laham: Rice with meat.

Khelwa: Isolation.

Kohl: Eyeliner.

Mahram: Impermissible.

Malcha: Engagement.

Masha Allah: God bless.

Meswak: Cleaning stick for teeth.

Misyaar Marriage: Temporary but official marriage.

Qadhi: The judge.

Qahfiya: A head cap.

Sharia: Islamic law.

Shisha: A smoking device also known as "narghile".

Shomagh: A head cloth for men.

Surat Al Dukhan: A verse from the Holy Qur'an.

Wald Halal: A legitimate boy.

Translator's Note

One of the barriers that often confronts the translator of a literary text, in particular fiction, is the obsession – to the extent of fear – with the cultural content in the source text and the arduous attempts on his part to transfer it with a sense of honesty and commitment to the target text, and with a hope to preserve its sense of appeal and acceptability to the recipient. The transfer of the cultural content is a responsibility that aches the mind and the heart of the translator. His choices are limited, either to be honest, which may also underline the author's narcissism, racism, patriarchal attitude or more. On the other hand, he can act freely with his additions, deletions, and fabrications.

Lawrence Venuti's tools of 'alienating/foreignising' might have worked years ago; a good example is Dryden's translation of Virgil's *Aeneid*, or Ibn Al Muqaffa's *Kalila Wa Dimna* (a collection of animal fables). But today, the translator is advised to seek the path of hybridity in translation, 'to innovate and surprise, to express new emotions and ideas, to reflect changing sociocultural realities'. (Simon, S. p. 49.) In other words, the aim is not only to transfer the cultural content into the target text but also to preserve some 'unwanted' utterances, phrases and taboos.

Victim 69

Victim 69 is a cultural-bound novel, diffused with signs, offensive utterances, intolerable customs, inhumane manners and more. Moreover, *Victim 69* unfolds a heartbreaking story of women at one time in the history of one country. It is a tragedy and at the same time a celebration, a resurrection of a new era that is about to welcome the role of women in society. Both leniency and neutrality in translation are the key issues in sustaining the cultural content of any translation process. In *Victim 69*, attempts have been made to transfer the cultural content in the source text into the target text agreeably and satisfactorily; it does not, in any way, distort or divert from the essence of the culture of the source text, nor does it cause any offence or rage to the recipient. *Victim 69* has been shortlisted as one of the winning novels in the Arab world but due to its outspoken and explicit cultural message that underlined the practice of customs and tradition in marginalising women and minimising their role in society, the novel was not permitted to be published in some Arab countries. I sincerely hope that the fuss related to the cultural theme of the novel will relinquish soon and the novel becomes accessible to most Arab readers.

Part One

Mrs. Warsaw

1

Most Miserable People Ascribe the Cause of Misery to Their Childhood...

As I was going through labour symptoms, I asked the driver, Baha, to prepare himself for a long, strenuous drive. It was Wednesday afternoon when I packed my little bags and took some of the requirements for the road. Then, I left hurriedly to Al Qassim. The Indian driver, Baha, set off without arguing; he just did as I asked. It did not take us long to reach the main road. Hours of pain were spent with labour contractions mixed with the fatigue of the road. I spent my time moaning in the back seat between laying down and napping undisturbed, except by recalling the memory that played the scenes of the wounds. When I sat up, I asked Baha about the distance we had covered. He gazed into my eyes through the mirror that was hanging in front of him, keeping silent until I repeated the question as if I had woken him up every time. He only understood by repetition.

Having covered nearly seven hundred kilometres of paved and unpaved roads and allies in urban and Bedouin areas, some of which were unoccupied, I arrived at the town of Rafhaa, exhausted. The journey exceeded the expected seven hours. On the city's outskirts, I rented an apartment in a three-storey building that looked half its age. I paid in advance for the rental of four full days. I asked Baha to look for his many acquaintances in the area to stay with them and not to come back until I called him. He shook his head, wetted his lips and left.

I made a phone call, the consequences of which would remain on my mind forever. A Bedouin woman answered quickly and briefly. I had communicated with her earlier about this critical intended assignment, the type of service that she was used to performing. In return, she had received a sum of half a million Saudi Riyals. After that terse call, an old, white 1.8 Hilux pickup, which was popular in those Bedouin areas, arrived. A skinny, tall, bent-backed man drove the vehicle. He tied his red *shomagh* around his face as a mask. Next to him sat a slim woman clothed in black from the top of her head to her toes. She removed the veil covering her face and used it as a mask, quickly hiding her face. She said it was for possible security precautions. I could not recall the features of her countenance except for a tattoo dot on the middle of her chin, a green tattoo locally known as *daq* or *daqqa*. The tattoo fixed the vision of that woman in the memory of whoever saw her forever; could it stay in my feeble memory?

The woman welcomed me very warmly. She spoke a Bedouin dialect. Her gold-plated teeth became apparent and her smile resembled a wolf impersonating a human. She helped me slowly to the back seat and pushed herself to the rear from the other door, saying, 'I am Um Humood, the midwife who talked to you on the phone some time ago. *In Shaa'Allah*, we will carry out what we have agreed without any problems.' Then she quickly ordered the slim driver to set off, 'Abu Humood, let us go.'

From there, we passed through streets, roads and various alleys that were levelled and twisted. The hot air and dry dust were hitting the car. Despite all these obstacles and conditions, the driver appeared experienced and knew the roads by heart. It seemed like he was used to it and had done the same tasks many times.

After half an hour, we reached a remote village. I read its name at the exit of the main road, Hijrat Aljabhan. Various houses, mostly white, some brown, were scattered at times and assembled at others. Most of them were old, built in the desert style. Many ragged tents, white and even black, spread between the ranches in many places, emitting disgusting smells occasionally.

The Hilux stopped in front of a house that seemed better off than its neighbours. After the dust had receded, the driver pulled up at the side of the house. The midwife got out, as light as a bee. She opened the door for me, and I leant on her; she helped me to get out and enter the modest building. She led me to one of the rooms near the main entrance with a metal gate. In the room, I saw some simple pieces of furniture, a white mattress and pillows. Um Humood made me sit opposite the window, which she covered with a short thick curtain. She closed the window tightly as if the residents abhorred the external light. Half of the lower parts of the walls were painted in light green while the upper parts of the walls were all painted in white. I noticed lots of sheets spread around here and there. Then, the woman talked in a voice full of maternal kindness, contrary to what I felt when talking to her on the phone, as if she wanted to comfort and reassure me and ease my mind over what I had spent for the mission; having spent all my savings and what I borrowed from the banks, amounting to half a million Saudi Riyals. That was all that I owned, the value of my jewellery and the bank loans.

They made me sit on a bed on the ground and fixed one of the pillows against the walls as a support, which made me feel comfortable. The woman, despite her self-composure, was agile and quick. I was amazed at her movement and gracefulness. She did not exhaust her energy and wasted no time. She gave me some water and hot soup. She ordered me to carry out her instructions by her facial expressions. As soon as I consumed the soup, Um Humood held my hand, pulled the pillow from behind me, and asked me to lay on my back and bend my legs. I wanted to forget the pain and took my mobile phone from my bag. There, I saw the photo of my children, Swar and Musa. I kissed the screen and looked at the clock, which showed 1pm.

After that, the midwife locked the room firmly, where the odour of the Dettol, some medications and herbs had turned it into a primitive operation theatre. She tightened her mask, and I lay on my back as she pulled my legs straight till the blown-up belly appeared. She wiped it gently, sensing it, then listened to the sound of the moving foetus. I lifted my legs from the knees, which formed a shape like a pyramid. She went down to the bottom of the pyramid, looking at its base to check how it was, then said, 'The womb is open.' She inserted her hand into the passage at the foot of the pyramid where the light of life came out of the darkness. She touched everything with her expert hand. Then, she poked with her inner thumb and tilted the head, checking the terrain. Then, licking her tongue, she said with great confidence, 'The head is now down; we need some time and then the labour will start, God willing. You must repent to God, my child, so the delivery becomes easy for you.'

I raised my voice, trembling with fear and announcing, 'I swear to Great God that it is a *halal* child, on God's way and his Messenger's, but his father betrayed me, yes, betrayed me. God is above the unjust. May God have revenge for me. Allah will help me, Allah suffices me, for he is the best disposer of affairs.'

Um Humood became silent for a while before asking me, 'What tribe are you from? Your dialect indicates that you are from a large family. I hope the baby is *halal*…'

I shook my head, refusing to disclose the name of my tribe.

Then, she added, 'Your looks and features are those of a descendant of a tribe, and your dialect indicates that, yes, indeed. We assist and help; we are here for the people.'

I did not give her a complete answer. I recalled the enormous amount of money that she asked for to accomplish this assignment. She then inserted a herbal suppository with her dry thumb, and I felt nothing. She mentioned that it was a suppository that would make me feel comfortable and enhance the labour process. She asked me when the last time I had had a meal was. I said it was a week ago. Um Humood rebuked me with swollen eyes and asserted, 'The labour pains are sharp, and your body cannot bear them. You have experienced giving birth twice.'

I yielded to her advice again. She brought me hot soup. I had a few sips, then reclined, waiting for the arriving one, with the will of God Almighty. Um Humood left the room, and I closed my eyes, recalling the stored memory as if I had met this woman before, but when and where? I felt sorry and dismayed for myself. The moment I held the mobile phone, she quickly returned, and I saw her standing by me, sighing. She placed her hands on her waist like someone expecting a catastrophe. She bit her lips and said, 'Your body is feeble. If you don't eat, you and the baby may die and delivery will be complex; it requires strength. Ya, you know that, and *Masha Allah* you have the experience.'

I did not answer her but held the phone and began to look at the photos of my children smiling. Swar was eight, and Musa was six. I didn't know why I saw the whole world in their eyes. I could see they knew where and what I was doing, but my mind said they did not know anything. I had nothing left in this world except them.

Um Humood examined me nearly every hour until midnight. The labour pains mounted, the pace of the womb's contractions increased, my screaming rose with the signs of delivery, and the course of action unfolded. Um Humood examined the foot of the pyramid and placed her hand there. She turned her rough thumb down there. She took it out and rubbed it against the top of her index finger. The moment she felt the stickiness of the liquid sprouting, she entered her head under the bedcover. She then pulled her head out again and called her assistant, 'Sister, prepare the warm water quickly. Labour has begun.'

The assistant, a fat, flabby, dark-skinned woman, entered and sat next to me, placing my hands on the floor and wiping them tenderly. Um Humood was working diligently to complete the mission. As the baby pushed its head, I felt my soul also coming out of my body. I held the phone as if I was clenching onto my life and hugging my children. I screamed until I was out of breath, and the baby uttered a cry, opening his window to life, sensing its light and breathing its air.

The midwife lifted his feet, saying, 'It's a boy, congratulations!'

I quickly retorted, 'I know it's a boy, and his name is Isa, and nobody can ever change his name.'

The midwife cut his umbilical cord, cleaned it and placed him on a white cloth beside me on the floor. She then changed the bed where I had delivered. I raised Isa to my bosom, and the milk overflowed from my breasts. Isa naturally searched for the milk with closed eyes. I put the nipple in his mouth and the secret of life poured inside him. I felt him sucking, trying to feel me with his little hands. This is how I thought of him, and nothing is more accurate than the feelings of motherhood. Isa sucked with closed eyes until he was satisfied. I prayed to God to bless him wherever he was. May God have revenge on those who inflicted injustice on both of us. God is most merciful, and we count on him.

Um Humood said, 'Don't seek God to take revenge, you good lass. God will be with you when you remove envy and revenge from your heart.' I did not respond to her but remained relying on God only. The midwife placed Isa beside me, on a white bed made of a sponge. The baby went into a deep sleep, and then Um Humood gave me a herbal medication with the soup that had an acrid taste. The womb's bleeding stopped a few minutes later. Then, I fell into a deep sleep, and I thought it was a short death. I woke up only after dawn. I found the woman lying down beside me. Her face seemed familiar. I tried to recall its features, but I couldn't. The minute I moved, she spontaneously woke up and put her mask on. I told her I wanted to return to my family, children and home.

She said, 'Impossible, your body is still weak. It can't bear any movement.'

Still lying on my right, I turned to her and said, 'I want you to call for the wet nurse right now.'

She said by way of introducing her, 'Her name is Um Rabi'a, and she is my sister. She is waiting outside.' She called her, and Um Rabi'a came in. She was the same dark lady wearing a mask. I did not understand why they were putting on the masks at home. She greeted us, looked at the newborn, and lifted him to her enormous bosom.

My heart hung with him, and my eyes followed them. I said, 'Feed him now in front of me. Let him have his fill, and later feed him twice daily when he is awake.'

The nurse laughed and giggled. She knew the secret and what was behind it. Um Humood said to Um Rabi'a, 'Um Isa wants to see you feeding her baby three times, and she knows that breastfeeding three times a day means that the baby is your son, and you are his mum. This is what Um Isa wants to see before she leaves. She just wants to be reassured and have her mind put at ease.'

The nurse laughed and inserted her nipple between Isa's lips, showing her ability and confidence in her motherhood. She stroked his head with her gentle hands while he was sleeping in her arms. She kissed his forehead behind the mask, and I felt her smelling him. I did not make eye contact with her. I repeated to Um Humood my wish to leave soon. After some insistence and a bit of stubbornness that I instinctively had, Um Humood reluctantly agreed, after rebuking me earlier. She asked me to stay for three nights to regain my energy.

It was morning and I was preparing myself to leave. Um Humood brought me hot soup and seven dried dates. She left me the meal and repeated her question, 'What tribe are you from? Your dialect is certainly familiar.'

'Al Samri tribe. Keep it secret. I promise you, I will not stop visiting Isa,' I said unpretentiously.

She had a deep, sudden breath as if she was sure of something still buried in her bosom. I saw her smile and something of contentment in her eyes. It was as though she perceived the meaning of the tribe and the principles of ethnic origin.

I took my son back to my bosom and smelled life in him. I hugged him for so long. In return, I made him cry, and he made me cry too. I mourned him, and he, in turn, also lamented me. I said to them, 'Never underestimate him. He is a legal offspring, *wald halal*. My blood and that of my forefathers are pumped into his veins. Tell him always that I love him so much. Tell him that I shall come back one day to take him officially. I want him to live with his brothers and me. He may also live with his father. I shall transfer cash to you whenever needed. You spend on him as much as I can afford. Don't be stingy with him.'

Then, she took him from me and gave him to her fat sister, two years her junior, she had said. She was overweight, flexible, and had heavy movements, unlike her sister. Nobody would ever bet that they were sisters. Um Rabi'a gave birth to her child one month earlier than me. She fed Isa again in front me and I reminded them both of the agreement that Um Humood would bring him up, and her sister Um Rabi'a would feed him.

I took the same Hilux back from Hijrat Aljabhan to Rafhaa. After another hard time and a long way on levelled roads and other winding ones, which the driver followed to avoid the security men and their questioning, I arrived at the apartment that I rented earlier in that remote area. I quickly gathered myself, wanting to wipe it off my memory, and collected my things. I then called Baha. Not before long, the driver called to tell me of his arrival. He waited for me by the building. He opened the back door for me and took me in my Corolla.

On the way to Al Qassim, I began to reminisce about past events as a resounding silence fell over me. A tape of past events ran through my mind with their alterations, all my calamities and setbacks. I recalled what I learnt in my philosophy and psychology courses: that most miserable people ascribe their misery to their childhood and history. This is a grave mistake that I should correct. From this very minute, I must live with the present and its crises, with Isa alone. Once again, I fell lost in the labyrinth of memory, with thoughts coming and others wiping them out.

At last, in the evening, we arrived at our big house in the heart of Al Qassim. Baha parked the car on the opposite side of the building. I went up to my apartment adjacent to that of my folks through the entrance on the private side. Baha left after I had signalled to him with my head.

I retired from the whole world. I just wanted to be away from humans and isolate myself for a while to rethink what had happened fully. I wanted to live by myself to maintain my independence. I always reiterate that an intelligent person is the one who supports his autonomy in a group. I admit now that I lack that quality. I remained in the apartment for a week, checking my body and retrieving my breath. However, illusions and nightmares never left me, and neither did the aspirations. I knew the only way to overcome pain was to understand how to bear it. That was how I expected the fast-forthcoming events to be. I may slip in them and perhaps fall and get drowned in them. I recalled what I repeated to my students about Freud: 'When you recall your memories, you would find that the years of hardship were the most beautiful years in your life.' I cursed Freud's theories and his nonsense.

I decided to see my mother at the family house adjacent to my apartment. The moment I greeted my mum, she said decisively, 'Your face is black! Oh my God!'

I stuttered then and all my words were lost. Perhaps I forgot to look at my face as I was remembering the angelic face of Isa. I didn't examine my face carefully in the past days. I forgot, which saddened me. How miserable you are, Warsaw! Isa's angelic face appeared in front of me; did I read his face as my mother read mine? Mothers' own strong abilities to consume their children's decisions in their presence and during their absence. I was afraid that Mum would know my condition without my revealing anything to her. What motherhood was this? If that happened, it was not bad and not good either. If she knew, she would relieve me of the burden of telling her, even if that resulted in expelling me from the family or mercilessly killing me. If she did not know, that was also good. Only then would things revert to normality rapidly. I would retain my relationship that I severed with my brothers intentionally to end the assignment of the birth of Isa.

I said to her, clarifying, 'The judge ordained the custody of my children to my divorcee. There could be nothing crueller on the heart of a mother. This is what made my face black, Mum.'

'Never mind, my child, a father's heart for his children is no less kind than the mother's. Remember that a father cannot not care for the children for a long time; he will send them back to your lap, don't worry,' my mum said.

I thanked God so much after my white lie worked on my mum. The whole story passed peacefully. I sat beside her and asked for some hot milk so I could relax by its warmth near my mother's kindness. I said, 'Mum, tomorrow I shall go back to the university. I shall return after the leave of absence and follow up on the custody with Abu Musa.'

2

Claiming the Truth Is Another Lie...

After ten days of attrition, signs of delivery pain began to diminish from my body while my soul remained in need of medication. But still a string of pain ran rampant through my throat to the liver. I wanted to take advantage of the beginning of the week, so I could return to the university after a six-week absence. I returned Swar and Musa to their father, asking them to be obedient to him. I drove with Baha to Al Qassim University, which I missed truly.

He opened the rear door, and I sat in the car, but he stood still in his place. I asked him to hurry up. He moved to his seat and began looking at me through the looking glass which was fixed in front of him. I shouted at him, 'Drive fast to the university.'

I went in dressed elegantly after choosing the most beautiful clothes in my wardrobe; bright-coloured clothes made by international brands that I intentionally wore to show off myself. I wanted to conceal my pain and cover up my broken soul by displaying my outer self well as much as I could. My only wish was to look sublime, stand erect and not to fall. I wore a scent of various fragrances that I had mixed, spreading a unique aroma into the atmosphere. I drew the *kohl* ostentatiously around both sides of my eyes in an almond or pecan shape to look like the eyes of the oryx, the wild Arabian gazelle. I used pink lipstick to match my dress that appeared under the *abaya* whenever revealed. As usual, I found Baha peeping through the mirror absent-mindedly. I pointed to him with my forefinger, making him understand my feelings before describing him with an epithet he wouldn't like to hear. I arrived at the university and registered my presence manually and electronically. I made it a point to shake hands with everybody and smile at them until I reached my office, where I lay down to relax. The academic day began smoothly, with no hiccups whatsoever. With all these crowded surroundings, I regained my confidence gradually and my ability to teach and argue convincingly. It seemed to me that insanity is deeply rooted in human beings. Usually, I try to hide my anxiety and tension by being in the crowd. It is, I believe, an attempt to evade facing madness vis-à-vis.

Life went on until Thursday of that unusual week. I received a phone call from the head of the department inviting me to join an online meeting at 9am. It was a virtual meeting with the academics of the two departments, male and female students. It was arranged by the Education Authority and the Higher Administration of Quality and Planning, via a large screen where we could see the professors sitting in the students' section. The university council held a meeting in the Conference Hall Platform, where the President of the University, the deans of colleges, the advisor general and other officials were present. The moderator gave a speech introducing the prominent personalities. He welcomed them, the professors and the administrators. He then let them speak according to their administrative status, not according to the seating arrangements nor the alphabetical order of names, as the tradition was in the previous meetings. Each one presented a detailed report about the hurdles met in the last term. The moderator ended by reading the recommendations that would feed into the outputs of university education policy. After that usual and boring introduction, the participants presented their achievements and addressed a mechanism for faculty evaluation and the items for the term evaluation. Then they discussed the university's official website and the college's web page, each contributing and presenting his vision.

At the end of the meeting, the platform was opened for enquiries and comments. With an impulse not new to me, I, as usual, asked to make the first comment. All eyes were up, chasing me as if some were waiting for me and others were watching me. Although unsure of what I wanted to say, I took the microphone. I expressed my wish to speak. I felt the urge to prove myself and record my presence. I said, 'I am Professor Warsaw, a lecturer of Psychology and Philosophy at Al Qassim University.'

I wanted, through my voice, to be myself, and not fear anybody; no one could see me but God alone. By praising Him, calmness and the flowing of life will be replaced, and confusion will diminish. However, a concerned man present in the audience recognised and observed me. That was what upset me and it was observed in my talk.

I felt it was the right time to confront him, face him, speak before him, and tell him that I was back at last. I came back as strong as I had always been, stubborn and holding on to my target. I returned to my position and my natural place despite all the obstacles and difficulties that he placed in front of me. He created those to make me leave the university. I fixed my eyes on the monitor and he recognised my voice. He was also upset, stuttering and blushing. All eyes turned towards me, watching my movements and what was hidden in me. I did not know precisely how all the people could distinguish a woman from her veil when nothing was apparent except the eyes. It seemed that the only way to distinguish and chase the veiled women was by constantly gazing into their eyes, as it was the only successful way to recognise women in a vast society like that. That habit moved to the university campus. Perhaps half of the audience knew me before I started my comments, but surely the rest could identify me later through my voice too.

I spoke hesitantly and was not conscious of what I was saying precisely. 'Brothers and sisters in the audience, it is a beautiful meeting that the university holds every quarter in the presence of the teaching team, the people, the president, and the deans of all colleges. We should not forget, of course, the university advisor, Dr. Abdul Rahman bin Isa. Yes, the Advisor is here. It is an opportunity for all to speak and say what they want. For all of this, I suggest documenting the field visits with the students on the web page of the academic staff – yes, documentation is one of his rights… Thank you, and peace be upon you all.'

The audience exchanged looks, stared at me, and kept blinking. They asked among themselves what precisely did this woman want to say. Then, the moderator intervened, putting an end to side talks. I did not know what I talked about, so I did not understand what the moderator said. I was staring into the eyes of the Advisor only. I noticed that he was sweating and kept changing the way he was sitting. He moved his *shomagh* left and right and scratched the tip of his nose until he took out the handkerchief to wipe the sweat from his forehead.

The meeting ended and I left quickly for my office, trying to regain my breath which was not at that time harmonious. I felt difficulty in breathing and acute chest pain spread to my liver. I fell on the office chair for a few minutes, not knowing what to do. Then I bounced at the sound of the office phone. A phone call came directly from the office of the dean of the College of Management Science and Humanities.

'Hello, Mrs. Warsaw, the dean wants you to come to his office immediately.'

'What is the matter?' I asked.

'You come now and then ask what you want,' he said.

I went to the office of the dean, and he received me himself. He stood up, greeting me, and asked me to sit down at the conference table. 'Professor (Mrs.) Warsaw, allow me to tell you about your professional records. You applied for a leave of absence, and the university did not approve it. You were absent for three weeks from the university without a logical or medical excuse. We are, therefore, obliged to suspend you from work and perhaps, later, dismiss you unless you produce a legal justification for your absence from work for three continuous weeks. The students' interests come first here, which is a high priority for us. These are the regulations and rules of the university, and nothing personal. I hope you understand my stance.'

I remained silent, as I knew the cause and who stood behind it. Before leaving the office, I was confident that the

Advisor of the University of Al Qassim was behind this, and he had notified the dean. The latter should pass orders to the director of human resources. My position at the university had now become critical, like the situation between the hammer and the anvil. I told him I was at the court of law, dealing with the case of custody and alimony.

He said, 'You must produce an official document before your teaching timetable is withdrawn and assigned to another lecturer and before your services are finally terminated. We are working on maintaining the quality and outputs of education, which are the essential reasons for our existence at this university.'

I asked the dean for a respite of three days to bring the legal excuse. By then, only a few weeks would remain before the end of the term, and I wouldn't be able to apply for leave without pay. I returned to my office, feeling shattered and marginalised in the true sense of these two words. I called the Advisor on his private number, but he blocked calls from my number. Then I called his office and asked his secretary to speak with him. In turn, she asked me who was calling. I gave her my name. She said she would transfer my call then. I waited in line, but she came back to tell me, 'His Excellency, the Advisor, is in an important meeting. Give me your full name and number so I can call you back later.'

I knew he would never call me back, as he feared confronting me. This fear shook his existence and respect and threatened his family, profession and social position. I left the college and went to a nearby shopping mall to change the telephone chip or the SIM card. I called again, and his confident voice came, 'Peace be upon you.'

'I need to meet you, otherwise I will come now to your office. You know well what I could do,' I said firmly.

'What do you want? What is your demand?'

'I delivered a child for you and gave him the name of Isa. I want you to recognise him, and I want to return to the university, and you know I was on maternity leave and have no official documents. You know that and you know all the causes. Understand?'

'There is nothing between us, Professor; this is the first time I've heard that a woman can conceive and give birth through a phone call.'

'Listen to me carefully. If you do not come this evening at six to the same place where we met the first time, I shall announce the news to all in the university and to your wife. As I said, I will destroy everything; let it fall on me as well as my foes. You know what my tribe could do, and you know the Bedouins very well.'

The time was five in the evening. I went to Rollins Al Qassim Hotel on the first floor. At the café, I sat next to a glass wall watching the main entrance. The Advisor came just five minutes before six. Unlike most of the hotel residents and the café customers, I saw him parking his car near the main gate.

Yes, the Advisor, Dr. Abdul Rahman bin Isa, entered the hotel lobby with his long *shomagh* dangling on his shoulders. He had his sunglasses on, covering half of his reddened face. I observed him as he entered quickly, avoiding looking at the people in case he might see any of his acquaintances. He knew well the table I was sitting at. He came and pulled the wooden partition behind him, making it a curtain. He sat before me without greeting me, unlike the acts of greeting he used to do a year and a half ago when he showered me with his presents and his honey tongue. I thought they were romantic at first. Now, they were nothing but a fraudulent act hiding behind it a foreseen betrayal. I wished he would show even half a smile. Soon, he began his conversation with an apparent anger. 'Warsaw, where have you been hiding all this time?'

'As if you didn't know! Yes, as if you didn't know, Bu Isa.'

His eyes widened, and he bit his lips and pointed at me with his short index finger. 'You know who I am, my position in the university, my family and society. I don't want to cause an uproar, and I don't want to hurt you either; no, I don't.'

I smiled sarcastically at his attitude and his hollow threat. He couldn't carry out any of his threats. He knew that if I told my family, he would be killed before I was dead too. He realised if his wife knew, that would destroy his family, and if the news reached the university, he would be fired. This was how I estimated the situation and saw it exactly.

I said, 'I want you to admit your fatherhood to Isa. If you can't, I need the *misyaar* contract between us. My son must be documented by an official legal document maintaining his future rights.'

The man softened his attitude and sat upright, placing his black spectacles on the table. 'Listen carefully to what I say. I shall handle all matters related to his documentation. He should be among his brothers naturally and officially. Warsaw, could you only tell me of his whereabouts?'

I smiled and was about to giggle. He wanted to know the whereabouts of Isa to kill him and erase all that implicated him. How could a mother hand her infant baby to his killer? 'Listen to me, please; you shall never reach him except after legally documenting his birth.'

That minute, he stood up and threatened furiously, 'I shall sack you from the university. As I said, I have never known that phone calls could beget children. There is no contract between us. What was between us was no more than phone calls, you slut! Bye!'

I bit my lip assertively, imagining that he was standing in front of me, saying, 'Your acting does not intimidate me; your appearance does not reveal if you own good or bad ethics, but your ability won't continue in this manner – changing colours like a chameleon – for long. Your pretending truthfulness is a short-lived lie, Doctor!'

3

A True Novelist Is the One Who Creates a Novel...

It was morning and the sky was cloudy. I was in great haste as if whatever I had learnt theoretically at the university now became a reality in front of me and applicable to me. We were told in psychology books that "active behaviour is self-escape", and during the activity you forget yourself and escape from your worries. I preferred that day to prove the validity of what I had prompted the students to learn and to prove that my day was eventful, which would make me forget my fears and wipe out the grief. I did not wear any makeup except mascara and powder foundation. I sprayed anbar and oud perfume on my *abaya*. I came out and saw Baha absent-mindedly leaning on the car door. I waved to him and scolded him for looking half asleep. I told him to move, and he drove directly to the family courts. There, I greeted anyone I met, displaying a broad smile to attract attention.

I wondered about the best way to attain what I wanted. I could find no weapon except that of femininity, which I had to express even if it was an exaggerated behaviour. I spoke to the employee on duty very briefly and softly in a way that most women know how to apply. I sat on his right side with my back to the rest of the employees. I went to him with all the femininity I had when I spotted him focusing on the lines of the *kohl* through the veil with the scent of oud and anbar, which are used all over Al Qassim. The man soon began to lose his balance. He brought his *meswak* out of his desk drawer and began to brush his teeth slowly. He soon regained his balance and was confident he could seize his valuable prey. He understood the insinuation, and I realised soon what he desired. Gradually, I caught him in the lethal femininity trap. I said to him very clearly, 'I need an official document proving that I visited the court daily last month.'

'Were you actually here at the court?'

'Not precisely, but could I have the official evidence or not?'

'At once, of course, my dear, this is peanuts, but…' The clerk inserted the *meswak* into his mouth and began brushing his teeth, turning his black lips into a small circle overlooking the outside. He asked me, 'May I have your phone number? Perhaps you may need me for something else.'

I winked at him with the side of my eye. The man was so glad. He handed me a piece of white paper where I wrote the number and gave it back to him as an official duty. He made a fast call immediately to be reassured of the number. Then, he raised his thumb as if making a fingerprint. Afterwards, he slumped in his seat and thanked God, saying, 'God be praised who made *misyaar* marriage *halal* and possible.'

The man was pleased with his catch, while his imagination ran wild. I repeated my order, 'One for one, measure for measure, an official document for a *misyaar*.' I asked him to produce an official document proving that I was at the court during that period. He took out an official sheet of paper and placed it in the printer. He keyed in the dates required for the visits. In his document, he stated that I visited the court every two days during the past three weeks.

He relaxed in his chair and placed his *meswak* on the table, and said, 'What is the number of the case, Professor?'

'Sixty-nine. Yes, case sixty-nine.'

'We need the stamp of the judge to document it officially.'

'OK, show me your mettle.'

He rearranged the position of his headkerchief *shomagh*, the headgear *iqal*, and buttoned his collar and left to visit the office of Judge Qadhi, which was located at the end of the corridor. He returned after barely five minutes with the stamped document. The groom returned joyfully with his hunt and placed it on his desk, tapping it with his index and middle fingers. Then he handed it over to me, proud of his achievement:

'You're precious, and your request is nothing much, Mrs. Warsaw. Here you are.' He gave me the official document with the signatures and the official government stamps that nobody could acquire easily. I took the paper and promised to call him the minute I left the door of the court.

'We could work together to attain many pending matters between us,' I said. The clerk was reassured, as he was filled with manhood. I left his office for the parking lot and found Baha browsing at photos on his phone. I told him to make a move, but he remained absent-minded. I hit him on the shoulder, telling him to move along quickly. He moved slowly. I called the clerk and promised him, 'Good news, we shall meet tomorrow in the parking lot after the end of the office hours. We shall agree on everything. You deserve every good thing. You did your best.'

I ended the call and went to the nearest phone shop to change the chip, and from that moment, I forgot about the clerk of the court (the man with the *meswak*). I called someone who mattered to me, though he never cared about me and waged a relentless war against me. I called the Advisor, Dr. Abdul Rahman bin Isa, who blocked any number from my phone. I called him directly and told him before he could hang up, 'Tomorrow, I shall return to the university against your will and with a piece of official evidence. Either you recognise me as your wife and Isa your son and…'

As soon as he recognised my voice and understood the threatening message, he hung up. I called him again, but he blocked the new number or switched off the phone altogether. He refused to talk to me and to recognise Isa as a legal and legitimate child born by the grace of God and His Messenger.

The following day, I entered the office of the dean, handed the secretary a personal letter with the attached report stamped by the court, and said sharply, 'Nobody has the right to suspend me from work.'

My academic life had returned to normal; however, my son Isa was not back to his life yet, as I was expecting. That is why I had to fight the world for his sake. Every mother is ready to confront the world for the sake of her children.

Many ideas and thoughts struck my mind, and I was still looking for effective ways to retrieve the legal rights to my child, Isa. At one time, I hoped to reach a man of a high official position, much higher than the Advisor. I wanted the Advisor to stoop down humbly, offering his confession. Here, I had two options: the first was that the man should be of a high office at the university or in the kingdom so that I could lure him, making him fall into my net. Then through him, I could twist the arm of this coward Advisor. However, this option would mean I would have to submit myself to this official to tamper with it as he liked. That would be another problem or catastrophe in this society. In my position, nobody would marry me except in *misyaar* marriage, another form of having a lover outside of wedlock. My experience in the past made this matter unattainable. It was impossible to submit my body to another man again after those experiences of which I admit their failure, especially my relationship with the Advisor who left a deep, incurable wound in my heart.

The second option was to expose him on social media or through literature. Yes, literature, and why not? He adored literature and had published some novels and other publications. There would be no harm if I sent him the message through a book or literary work. There was the novel, a widespread genre in recent years. So why don't I try my luck at writing a story to expose this Advisor? Then this would be a realistic genre of literature. Through this form, I could depict this society, the way of life, and its tradition, the good and bad things we inherited.

I began another mission and that was searching for a writer to help me write a novel. I could relate my story and put it in a literary text. Or I could write my story, and he could do the editing. I surfed Facebook, searching for "The Gulf Novel". Many sites and names of interested writers and critics, known and unknown, appeared. At one point, I focused on critics and excluded those from Saudi Arabia. It would be preferable that I shouldn't be locally known. There might be some whom I was acquainted with. I thought that the furthest I went, the better it was.

My choice fell on a critic from Bahrain called Dr. Sa'ad, who had published several books as a critic. I decided to communicate with him, unsure whether he would respond, I didn't know if he would help me. I wrote to him:

Asalaam Alykum, Dr.,

I am Warsaw from Al Qassim and I am currently writing a novel. As this is my first attempt, I need your assistance to provide your opinion and suggestions. If that is agreeable, I shall send you by email whatever I write, or any other methods you prefer.

Thank you very much.
Warsaw.

I returned to visit my mother, whom I missed talking to so much. She took me to her bosom, asking about my children's situation and the latest in the corridors of the court. I reassured her that things were alright and with the blessings of God and I would meet Swar and Musa on the weekend. I left her in the evening. Before I placed my head on the pillow, I did ordinary things, surfed the net and browsed Facebook, Twitter, Instagram and Telegram. I had a good surprise. The first response from Dr. Sa'ad came with his readiness to read my work and give me advice according to the school of criticism he followed.

I did not know about the school he was following or the method he would talk about. He asked me to send him all that I had written so far. But I had nothing to send, as I had written nothing so far. I replied to him saying I was about to write and would check the spelling and the grammar of the text, and then he had to check the narrative critically to establish if the average reader would enjoy it. I was a bit scared of the word criticism and I thought that it meant he would find faults with it and despise it. Then I remembered my personal problem and I set aside my fear; the goal was more important. I expected that the project would be a serious and effective way to bring back the rights to me and my son, Isa.

The following day, I began writing chapters of my tale as scattered headnotes. I expected that this would be accepted at the beginning. I sent him all of those. A day later, his brief comment came:

Good morning, Mrs. Warsaw,

You have an excellent literary sense, and I suggest you continue writing. I would ask you first to write your biography from the beginning so we could call what you wrote a "profound biographical novel". Remember that you are on the first step, and there is a vast difference between writing and creating a novel. Now, you are writing a novel, while a true novelist is the one who creates a novel. We shall cooperate and write a novel together. Write the first chapter about your childhood, family and parents. Then, we shall discuss how we can deal with the footnotes that we would delete at the end of the text. I want to invite you to visit Bahrain whenever it is convenient. Let us meet at one of the cafés so I can be sure that the woman I am dealing with is a literary woman and, further, to seek the truth of feelings through the expression of your body by reading you through the words you wrote or didn't write yet. If we agree on this procedure, we should begin our discourse immediately. Let us think of a kick-off next week.[1]

Regards, Saad.

I received Dr. Sa'ad's comments and all I longed for was to relate my stories in a book that would shake the Advisor. This would be a glimpse of hope and life for Isa. Perhaps I could bring him a smile through his father's recognition. He has the right as a human to live with his parents and his siblings. This step may not be decisive but would represent another sign of pressure to achieve justice.

In his later correspondence, Dr. Sa'ad said that writing about the stages of my personal life should represent a biography or a horizontal novel. I did not precisely know the essence of that kind of writing, but I had to try my best, and he had to correct the approach as an experienced critic. I agreed to write his comments in the footnotes on every chapter that I began as a narration, and then I would make amendments after the end of all chapters. Ultimately, we would delete the footnotes and retain the original literary text as a novel. That was how the agreement was concluded. Let's hope for the best.

---

[1] Creative Warsaw, it would be lovely to know that epistolary literature is an ancient art that changed in its old form due to the technological revolution and this is what has also caused changes to all literary expressions. Emails replaced the conventional paper mails due to its ability to be brief and due to its ability to be widespread. You possess the innate ability to narrate and your launch wasn't bad. I congratulate you on this successful step. Sa'ad.

4

Self-Revelation Reduces the Effects of Pain...

After I began writing the novel that I had called *The Victim*[2] and had already returned to work at the university on a regular basis, I had to return to my mother's lap and listen to her tales and sufferings in life. I had to add what she had revealed from her whole life to my knowledge. In other words, I was looking for the events which my eyes did not see and to document the highlights in her life and the events that she heard of. Altogether, I wanted to add to my total knowledge of the biodata of my mother. That was what

---

[2] Professor Warsaw, this is my first comment on your texts. To start with, I found the title carrying the word "Victim". I regarded it as a tentative term and we could add it to the list of suggestions. You should know the attributes attached to a successful title, so we could at the end choose the most appropriate one. The title should be neutral and should not reveal the text directly. However, I did not find neutrality in this title because it would drive the recipient to sympathise with the narrator as a victim and that would be a preconceived judgement contrary to the alphabet of the narration. My dear, a title is a semiotic indicator at the same level as a commercial advertisement, which aims to attract and influence the tendency of the recipient. Sa'ad.

Dr. Sa'ad had asked me to do before embarking on writing itself.[3] Thus, I began in the name of God.

I got used to having Friday breakfast with my mother for a long time, especially when my children spent the night with their father. I seized that opportunity to ask her about her life story from childhood. How could I begin with her without making her feel that I intended to record what she would say? In other words, to disclose herself without being observed, to be as she was totally in her loneliness and in my company. I said to myself, *I must catch her at the right time.* Soon, there was success and I had what I wanted.

In the beginning, the day was serene, and I entered the room as she was preparing breakfast to the sound of music of Fairuz singing. She stood at the oven, her words following the tunes and catching up with Fairuz, as if she was singing after my mother. I placed my hand on her shoulder silently; she trembled and quickly switched off the recorder. She looked behind her, taking a deep breath.

I asked her, 'Mum, you're still afraid of my grandfather and you are listening to the music.'

'God have mercy on my father; he did the impossible to stop me from hearing songs, but it was useless to me.' My mother laughed, and her laughter always had something that fascinated the place. I asked her to sit on the floor so we could have the breakfast together. She sat, relaxed, humming Fairuz's song.

---

[3] Professor, I thank you for your understanding and your good-heartedness in taking my notes seriously. You are now at the stage of constructing the characters, so that the recipient should absorb them socially and psychologically, and even the extent of their ability to explore their attributes and to move the destination of the following events. A clever step means a lot of things. Sa'ad.

Victim 69

I winked at her and said, 'Cream, Mum? And like what my grandfather used to say, "Derrida, honey."' The opportunity became appropriate when I sat next to her and said, 'What's my grandfather's story with the radio and songs, Mum?'

She sipped from the teacup, sighed, and began to tell her story. As I listened attentively to her, the vision of Dr. Sa'ad appeared in front of me and behind him I visualised that of the Advisor in the shape of a Devil.

She said, 'I was fourteen when your grandfather, may God have mercy on his soul, came one Friday evening asking to see me alone in his room. I still remember his features whether sad or happy. I entered the room; his eyes were bright, as if he was hiding his smile. His beard was thick in his youth, but still retained its colour in old age. He said, "My daughter, Hessa, you know that a woman has got to get married, and now, you have become a woman and a Derrida, you must get married. A young man from Al Qassim has proposed to you; he is a teacher, and I made enquiries about him, and he has no faults. I asked his family to come and ask for your hand next week. God bless you, my daughter. Thank God for everything." Yes, Warsaw. That is how your grandfather brought up the marriage issue; I accepted it without any discussion. That was how I got married for the first time. My husband and I moved to Riyadh, where he worked as a teacher in one of the government schools. Life there was different from Al Qassim's; I could breathe life there, far away from the strictness of Al Qassim. I gave birth within five years to your brother, Adel, and his two brothers. Meanwhile, I kept myself busy and took up an occupation in sewing, which was profitable, and my customers varied in class, until I was able to reach the high-class customers and even to the princesses.

'One day, Abu Adel returned from the school to join the children and me for lunch. He asked me how things were going on. I replied without hesitation, "As you were aware, Abu Adel, in Al Qassim, they forbade me from attending government school, and we had no choice but to participate in religious education only. Now, I feel so empty, more than any other time, when you go to work and the children to school. I have made up my mind to enrol in adult education programmes."

'He nodded, knowing that I was simply informing him and not expecting a decision or response from him. After that, my days were busy as the children and their father went to school while I made dresses all morning, prepared lunch, and after that, attended adult evening classes.'

My mother gave a deep sigh. 'By God, those were my happiest days, Warsaw; I was Derrida, as your grandfather called me, very beautiful until, that cursed day.'

My mother had an exciting narrating style; with her voice fluctuating up and down according to the words' meanings, forcing the listener to be attentive to her. I let her speak.

'That day, your grandfather arrived unexpectedly from Al Qassim with a new project for my husband, a small shop that would bring him an extra income, he said. But when he returned in the evening, he did not find me and asked your brother, Adel, who was a child, "Where is your mother, son?"

"At school." I still remember how your grandfather received me at the door. I greeted him, but he shouted, pulling the books from my hand as he roared, throwing the books on the floor. Then he asked, "What are these, Hessa?"

"Textbooks and exercise books." Your grandfather began tearing the books as if they were his enemies and wanted to take revenge.[4]

'He remained screaming while tearing the books, saying: "God save me, oh you devil, go away, you filth." He asked me if I had more of the books, which I completely denied.'

I denounced the term *Jelf*, meaning filth. I heard it from my mother for the first time and asked for its meaning. She said my grandfather used that word whenever he did not like something, and it meant the Devil or a madman. He used Derrida for anything beautiful, especially when describing a woman.

My mother did not mention where her father got these words. However, she continued her tale. 'Your grandfather went to my room, searched my wardrobe for a forgotten piece of paper wrongly hidden in my clothes, and there came the great calamity.'

I asked my mother what my grandfather found in the wardrobe; my fear was that the next would be a scandal.

'Your grandfather found a small radio.' My mother laughed, showing her white teeth and the roundness of her cheeks. She asserted that then she was fond only of Um Kulthum and Abdul Wahab and did not like Fairuz. My mother continued, drawing me to listen to her. 'Your

---

[4] Warsaw, you are the daughter of Al Qassim. I very much admired your use of the rude word "*Jelf*" and "Derrida" as they are derived from the local environment. Each one has two meanings; one is obvious, but it is not the intention, and the other is hidden, but desired; this is called cultural innuendo. From what I have read from your writings, it seems to me that your name is a pun and your tale is a pun too, and therefore I must be a good critic to attain to what is intended. Sa'ad.

grandfather thought of the radio as the Devil and books or learning as the road to the Devil, the gateway to atheism. These are an abomination of Satan's work. He broke the radio into pieces and burnt it with the leaves of the books that evaporated with the smoke. Then he turned to my husband, Abu Adel, "Don't let her go to school. If you can't stop her, send me a letter."

As much as this situation made me laugh, it provoked me. I asked my mother what she thought of my grandfather's speech.

'If Satan were on the radio, he would have been burnt, and we would have got rid of him. The problem with the real Devil was the one nestling in your grandfather's head, the one roosting in the man's mind. Right or not?'

My mother leant on the back cushion in the middle of the hall, where she used to relax when sitting on the floor. I poured her a cup of coffee and presented her with some dates. She asked me about the explanation for that condition that swept my grandfather's mind whenever he saw something new. I dug into my memory, trying to remember some of what I studied in philosophy and psychology at the university. I found that it was a phobia or fear of everything new.

I said, 'Usually, Mum, anything new is confronted by an objection and a refusal in closed or conservative societies. This happened to you with the advent of the radio, microphones, and televisions. The clergy banned it as a taboo for the fear of the disintegration of the society and going out of the ordinary. This happens in all cultures.'

I asked her to forget both the college lessons and continue to the most crucial stage in her biography.

'When the storm receded, I sent for my neighbour, asking her to register me as an external student. My plan was to study here and be examined there. The school agreed. Then I gave her one hundred Riyals to buy me a new radio. I got it, and my life returned to normal. Thank God for that.'

Then, realising I was Warsaw,[5] I said to my mother, 'Did the news reach my grandfather in Al Qassim?'

'Your grandfather arrived suddenly from Al Qassim less than a year after his last visit. He greeted us and went directly searching for more filth, or the banned and tabooed. The radio and the books were at the side of the bed. What added to his fury was the knowing of your mother's husband, Abu Adel, of those forbidden things at his home. My father repeated the same act of breaking and burning the Devil and looked at the smoke of the forbidden stuff rising in the house. Then he paused, threatening, "Filth and *haraam*, this would be my last visit to your house; if ever I found any filthy forbidden things here again, I won't be your father, and you're not my daughter until the Day of Judgement."[6]

---

5   Mrs. Warsaw, any reader can notice that you are using more than one narrator in this chapter, which is critically disagreeable, but praiseworthy to the recipient on condition that they do not create a cover or confusion. On my part, I consider it necessary to unite the narrator in each chapter. It's your first experience and there's no harm in it. I could feel your ability to overcome the mistakes, which I hope you will rewrite or whitewash the text before printing. Sa'ad.

6   Mrs. Warsaw, it is preferable to use quotation marks for the dialogues said by characters directly. You may use one of the following formulas in your narration:
    'He said, this would be my last visit to your house.'
    'He said, it would be his last visit to our house.'
    He said, it would be the last day I visit your house.'
    Incidentally, I won't be using "Professor" anymore; however, your

'Thus, my daughter, Warsaw, I raised the white flag and dropped the handkerchief as proof that that would be the last time I would join formal education. I gave up studying just two months after obtaining the General Intermediate Certificate.[7] The final cycle of my life with my first husband had arrived. I do not deny that he was handsome and elegantly dressed. Having obtained a scholarship to study in Egypt, and having spent less than a year there, the great catastrophe came; your mother's husband fell prey to an Egyptian girl whom he knew and fell in love with. Since then, his travels to Cairo had been at the expense of his home and family responsibilities. He waited for her for a long time and travelled a lot, and finally married her in Cairo and returned with her boastfully to Riyadh. He rented her an apartment not far from mine. After that, he expressed his desire to spend one night with me and the other with her. As you are aware, the woman's heart never accepts a partner.'

I interrupted her, smiling, 'Is this what they call love, which forces a woman to refuse the presence of a rival?'

'No, no, Warsaw. This is the love of possession; we don't accept anyone sharing a room with us in a hotel. How could a woman share with us the heart of the same man?' My mother smiled, had a sip of her coffee, and continued. 'I sent a message to my father asking him to arrange a divorce. My divorcee did not mind, as if he were waiting for this time of relief; an obstacle which was removed from our path. I took your brothers and

---

status will be always reserved. Wish all barriers would fall and the writing be from soul to soul. Sa'ad.

[7] Warsaw, it is always said that redundancy is like deficiency and rhetoric it is the deletion of meaning as little as possible. Here, the repetition is irrelevant: if we delete one of the similes the meaning will not be affected; that is your choice. Sa'ad.

left for my father's home in Al Qassim. We were back in the same place where we are now. I found some relaxation in your grandfather's attitude as he became more tolerant, as if he felt guilty about agreeing to my marriage to that man.'

'How?' I asked her.

She laughed as she was talking, and then her voice dropped until it sounded downhearted. 'After obtaining my divorce, I saw a bit of remorse in your grandfather's eyes and I did my best to seize that opportunity. I complained of lethargy and the need for extra income. He agreed, and I resumed my old dressmaking hobby. He did not mind, and I was encouraged to acquire a new radio. I missed the songs of Um Kulthum, Abdul Wahab, and later Fairuz and Warda. When grandfather entered the house, he had the habit of clearing his throat to signify his arrival. I would hurry to switch off the radio. I swear to God, I did not hear his whining that day. He was furious again. He snatched the radio, threw it onto the ground and hit it with a large piece of rock in a dramatic, comic scene.'

My mum made me laugh by acting these dramatic scenes, moving her hands and feet to enact the meaning of her words. 'Thus, your tale ended with the radio, or the Devil, and the largest filth in Al Qassim,' I said with a smile.

She continued, 'It never ended. I had to buy other sets many times, which amused your uncles. I remember that your uncle and his wife paid us a visit to stitch a new dress for her.[8] I took her inside to photograph the outlines of her

---

8   Warsaw... do we have to stich an old dress? You better be as economical as possible in your words. I suggest you drop the word "new" as you will be omitting a lot of vocabulary and structures until the meaning is fulfilled. Writing matures with

body to cut the material accordingly. I finished the dress in two weeks and sent her the photographs after developing and printing the film. Then the hurricane blew from my brother's home. My brother went to my father and told him about the hideous crime I had committed – the sinful act of taking photos. As usual, my father was furious and tore up all the pictures and shouted in his usual manner about filth and the Devil. Also, your uncle tore his wife's dress into pieces. Then came their decision to marry me off so that sin would not be spread. Can you imagine, Warsaw, this was what happened?'

'Who was the lucky chap? Was it my father's turn?' I asked her.

'Unfortunately, your father's turn had not yet arrived. One customer from Al Qassim wanted to know my opinion about marrying her brother, who, she said, was a lecturer at the Islamic University. He was married and wanted me according to the norm of God and his Messenger.[9] She praised her brother so much, and I decided to meet him before saying yes or no. She conveyed that to her brother, who went to my father at his shop. Your grandfather met him and told us the story of that man from Al Qassim who wanted to propose to your mom, Hessa, but your grandfather instead went to close the shop door in front of him. The man understood that as my

---

experience, and you are now maturing on a quiet narrative fire. Sa'ad.

9   My dear… if we don't mark the dialogue with quotations, then we must be sure of the grammatical integrity. There is a grammatical error in the use of the word 'father' in your sentence above; it should be a possessive noun with an apostrophe (') –" father's". Therefore, quotations protect the dialogue from the critics as your clothes protect your body from stalkers. Sa'ad.

father's refusal to his proposal. He was dismayed and asked for the reasons. Your stubborn grandfather refused to talk to him except in a sign language. The man did not give up and repeated the attempt many times. And your grandfather was like a mountain that remained steadfast and firm in his position. The man decided to write letters and to place them under the shop door. Your grandfather would tell us, "What does this man with a shaven beard want? What should we do with his diplomas; this filth – doesn't he know that he who disobeys tradition has no place among us, and we do not want his certificates either?"

'Your grandfather was cross with him and wanted to end this farce. He met him again, hoping it would be the last time. The discussion was wide open. The man and his brother arrived, and they were so sure of themselves.

'The man said, "Ibn Baz allowed the legal meeting before marriage; why do you forbid it?"

'Your grandfather said, combing his dark black beard, "Go to Ibn Baz and ask his beautiful daughter for a legal meeting. He has a very (Derrida) beautiful daughter, marry her if he agrees."

I jumped up laughing and saod, 'And now came my father's turn. Is that right?'

My mother laughed and said, 'I don't wish your fate would be like mine, Warsaw. You are the most beautiful Derrida in the entire world. I am genuinely concerned about you among all your siblings.' Then, she continued narrating her tale as I tried to take her back to the past, but warning me after seeing my stubbornness that I had inherited from her.[10]

---

10 Dear Warsaw, it seems that I am working with a charming lady according to your mother's description – Derrida, as she likes to

'After that, your father came to propose to me. He is from the Samri tribe, as you know, which extends from Southern Iraq to Hael. He wanted me to be his second wife. Unfortunately, I had no wish for him because of his illiteracy, ignorance and incivility. Additionally, he was married to an Iraqi woman from Shammar, and had three boys and six girls. I recall that his firstborn was *Jelf* (filth), and his name was Fattal. I firmly refused your father, but your grandfather had the final say. In the end, I married him against my will.'

I laughed at her description of Fattal as filth. Now, we have two epithets: the filth of my father and my mother's Derrida. I asked about the reason. 'Mom, you asked for a divorce after your first husband married an Egyptian. Now, you accepted my father, who had nine children; among them, I know Fattal the filth, Abdul Rahman and Sa'ad. Why is this a contradiction?'

My mother continued narrating her tale. 'There, the first time I was the first woman and for the second woman it is always hurtful. Now, I became the second, that is, the hurtful, not the hurting one; that is why I accepted the proposal and don't you ever forget that I was divorced. In a tribal community, a divorced woman has no right of choice. I had to get married, my dear.'

---

say – and by God, I hope to see you soon. I may be flirting with you. However, let's go back to text. The flashback that you now are using is useful for knowing the characters of the novel and diving into their depths, but it usually slows down the speed of the events, as is happening with your mother now. You note here that the main events have come to a complete halt, and the reader has been introduced with you to the characters and circumstances that have been formed and influenced your personality. As a result, your overall behaviour has emerged, which will be shared with the reader later. I think you should redraft this chapter but not go beyond the general context. Sa'ad.

'And you had to give birth to me and put me in trouble in this world?' I said jokingly. My mother moved to live with my father in Al Qassim, where my father built two attached houses. The first was for his Iraqi wife, Um Adel, and the second for my mother, Um Abdullah, and he placed a back connecting door between the two houses to spend the night with each of his wives.

She said, groaning, 'Imagine, my love, I'm the second, and after me came the third, a widowed cousin of your father. I am the daughter of the Head of the Authority in Al Madina, but considered the third wife to your illiterate Bedouin father who could not read or write! He slept in a tent or in an animal shed, it didn't matter to him.' My mother refused to share the bed with him or let him touch her on the wedding night. She was disgusted with his smell, so she fled to my grandfather's home, who forced her to return to her husband's home. My father was very patient with my mother and never ceased expressing his love and fondness to her. This softened her heart, which was previously as solid as a metal.

She lowered her head to the ground to hide her tears after this bitter confession. I tried to make it up to her. 'Mum, the more you reveal what's inside you, the more the effect of the pain will dissipate.'

She promised to end her tale next Friday. I bid farewell to her with a kiss on her head and returned to my apartment to jot down my mother's words.

5

In Composing, Things Are Reconstructed in a Different Manner…[11]

I was in the final years of the primary stage of school when Saddam Hussain invaded Kuwait. The news that Saddam Hussain's aim was to liberate Palestine spread among the aged and the young. My father heard of Saddam's great aim with mixed feelings, and I didn't know how to describe them precisely, but he said to my mother while I was listening to him, 'Hessa, at last, someone came who wants to liberate Palestine.'

---

11 My dear, I notice here your insistence to stick to the timeline events; it began by your detaching your mother, and then your childhood and I expect the next will be about your first marriage and so forth. Perhaps this reflects your type of thought in dealing with the other. And I may say that this clarity is one of the reasons for the tragic ending in which you have fallen in and we try to find a narrative solution for it. That's how I read you. As far as your commitment to timeline narration is concerned, it is a traditional type. The writer's ability and distinction will be fully expressed when there is a leap over the timeline while preserving the events' connection. This is regarded as a kind of innovation and narration capability which takes away monotony from the readers. Looking forward to knowing what your writing will be after taking down these notes. Soon we will meet. Sa'ad.

My mother answered him sharply, an attitude she inherited from her father, 'Liberating Jerusalem doesn't come through occupying Kuwait. What if he entered Saudi Arabia as he claims? Should he proceed to Palestine or stay here to rule and order? He is an evil man and looks at all people as devilish like him.'[12]

My father clapped his palms as a sign of annoyance, and his mind somersaulted as if he was convinced by what my mother was saying. 'I think you're right, Hessa.'

It was been long before we began to see group migrations; people from everywhere fled out of fear of Saddam. The leader threatened to use chemical weapons if the allies attacked him. Tribes spreading in the desert to the South of Iraq, Kuwait and Saudi Arabia began to move southward. The kingdom opened its borders to all the displaced, and the Saudis opened their doors to accommodate them. As the Sameri tribe stretched from Southern Iraq to Kuwait, reaching into Hael and Al Qassim, and according to my Uncle Hamdan, which was confirmed by my father, the Samaris then had no option but to find refuge with their relatives, in those areas far away from the war zones and destruction. There were group migrations like I had never seen.

Crowds poured into our areas, and my father opened his house to receive all from our tribe, the Sameri. He divided

---

[12] I admit now that your beauty has moved to your language and became more mature and waiting for someone to pick it up. It's irrefutable to mention that narrative language emerges at two levels: the narration level, where the language is eloquent, flawless, and prestigious. The second is the dialogue level, where the language is low, colloquial, and falling. This is your choice: an eloquent and solid language or a common sweet dialect. I find you moving between the two according to the location. Sa'ad.

our house into two: the first floor for women and the ground floor for men. After only one week, the place was packed. Some families hung curtains as barriers inside the yard outside the house, while others erected tents adjacent to the homes as if those were caravans.

I didn't exclude any of the guests from sharing my little room. My mother asked me to host two girls; one was dark and grumpy, and the other was slim and pleasant. She introduced them to me, wishing that they would feel at home. I welcomed the two guests and introduced myself as Warsaw Bint Khalaf Al Sameri.

The dark one smiled sarcastically, saying in the form of a question, 'What's this? Is your name Warsaw? Haven't you found other names?'

I laughed a lot to avoid embarrassment, for I was used to announcing my name when asked by someone for the first time. My answer always remained as it is in any situation, 'May God forgive me mother, she does not want anything to adopt from her Bedouin ancestors, not even names. She was the one who chose my name, so she should be judged by God on the Judgement Day. Anyway, we need only a name to be called by others, a name to be introduced, and after all a name is not part of us.'

The slim one smiled, asking, 'You're Khalaf Al Sameri's daughter, owner of this house, and Hessa is your mother?'

'Oh, yes.'

They exchanged looks as if we agreed on a clandestine matter that they didn't want me to know. The slim one said, 'We're also from Al Sameri tribe, and this is my sister, two years younger than me. We won't tell you our names until we decide to return to Rafhaa.'

Victim 69

The dark one, I mean the younger one, said, 'We'll move your bed aside and sleep on the floor here.'[13]

The slim one sat on the floor as I was looking closely at her. She placed a green tattoo dot in the middle of her chin and tied a black band on her forehead which nearly concealed her eyebrows. She appeared to look like a Bedouin of twenty years of age, well-built despite her slimness. Her face was triangular with a rounded chin where the green tattoo was placed. She looked at her sister who said, in turn, 'We are from the Sameri tribe from Rafhaa villages; we may be closely related to you, or perhaps far, but we will tell you at the appropriate time.'

At that time, I recalled my mother's urgent request to welcome the guests and meet their requirements without putting any pressure on them. I wished them a quiet stay until the crisis ended with the return of Kuwait, or expelling Saddam, and even killing him. They smiled as if they thought I was a child in grade six. Perhaps they didn't want to chat with a child. I preferred talking about what they wanted throughout their stay with me.

It was November 1990 and I was on my return from the school, which was near our house. I found that the number of people in the house and outside had doubled. The streets were packed with cars and pedestrians. I entered the house using the back door and saw women crying and others comforting

---

13 Sometimes, I feel that there is more dialogue than usual here and I think the high quantity of the use of dialogue is because of two reasons: either the writer's attempt to flee from a difficult position in analysis and description, or that the writer is still in the early stage of writing. Since you are writing your first work, it's harmless if you take down this remark for your future work. Sa'ad.

them as if we were in a mourning gathering. I saw my brother, Abdullah, in the corridor that separated the *majlis* from the house. He approached me as if knowing what I wanted.

He pulled me and returned me to the corridor. He was about to talk, but tears fell from his eyes. I was afraid of what was in store for us and asked him, 'What's wrong with you? What happened, Abdullah?'

'Our brother, Adel, died in the war, Warsaw.'

My father held a condolence gathering in our house, as my uncle, Hamdan, did the same for the Bedouins at their location. I don't know why we fail to see the good deeds of others except after their death. My brother's life began to unfold in front of me like a screening tape: he was a handsome young man, educated and self-confident, an aviation engineer – what more? Everything in him was beautiful, even the day he passed away.

The Sameri tribe from Iraq, Kuwait, Hafre Al Baten and Al Qassim gathered for his funeral.

I asked Abdullah to find my mother among the women to ask her what we should do. My mother recommended that I should remain with the women, be hospitable to them, and condone my stepmother, the Iraqi Sameri wife.

Before the evening prayers of that day, the crowds dissipated. Some went far, others went to their tents. As for me, I went to see my father in his *majlis* with his dates and coffee. Some of my brothers were with him, and I didn't know their names. Some were from Al Qassim, Hael, and others were from Rafhaa and Hafre Al Baten. He asked me to sit beside him to introduce me to them.

'This is your sister, Warsaw, the chatterbox, the most beautiful Derrida, according to her grandfather.' Then he pointed at me and said, 'These are your brothers from your father's wives. My first wife was Iraqi Sameri; the second, your mother, a Tamimi; and the third, my cousin from Al Qassim.'

Some of them smiled, one welcomed me and one of them was busy speaking. 'You all know that Adel was an aviation engineer. He was on a mission checking a military aircraft, which is why a bomb exploded on board the plane and he was martyred, may his soul rest in peace.'

Another one said, 'It means Adel was killed, and Saddam did not reach Palestine.'

I saw anger on the faces of my uncle, Hamdan, and my father. Their eyebrows rose and the lines on their brows turned alike at the time of anger. My uncle said to all present in a voice that I can still remember, 'Adel's blood won't cool off except by Saddam's blood or one of his family's – one for one.'

Two months after that painful event, the blueness of Al Qassim's sky turned black as if it were the Day of Judgement. The sky nearly rained smoke. I recalled the *Surat Al Dukhan* as fear overcame the whole of Al Qassim region. I went to see my mother, fearing what was in the store for us and fleeing from the darkness of the day. She said, 'You thank God, Warsaw, if the situation aggravated, it means the relief will be near.'

The war broke out and we saw the planes, on television and radio, the bombs, rockets, and explosions that lasted long, and the day turned into night and the night into terror. As my mother expected, the news reached everywhere

Months later, my father placed the radio at the centre of the *majlis*, moving between the BBC and the First Saudi Channel. The definite news came of Saddam's army fleeing and evacuating from Kuwait. The danger was away from Saudi borders, and the Kuwaitis were waiting for the return of their Amir, Jaber Al Ahmad.

The migrants were hopeful and the tribes started packing in expectation of the return to their homes. They seemed to be in a hurry. Everybody wanted to be reassured about his home and property. They all returned, but my brothers were delayed at the wish of my father. The two girls remained in my room. I greeted them while they were talking about Saddam and Palestine. With her withered face that looked dry as an arid land, the skinny girl said, 'Warsaw, your father Khalaf Al Samri had twenty-eight children from three wives. Some of them live very far away. It would be nice if they all met on happy occasions next time.'

The skinny girl was a bit upset while packing, while the other one remained, biting her lower lip. I wanted to help them. The younger one said, 'My sister, Jaza'a, and I should go. However, we should try to meet at better times. It would be nice to act as your hostess the way you hosted us.'[14]

---

14 Dear Warsaw, I've spotted your ability to select the right words and structures as if you are choosing what suits your beauty. Referring to this reporting sentence perhaps is emerged and diverted from the narrative context of the text. This is a repeated error in your case. You must narrate the events without being engaged emotionally; the more the narrator disappears, the more successful the text is. Remember that creativity is fulfilled when you are like a corridor through which things pass so you don't have to stand an obstacle in front of it. I hope when we meet you are relaxed, and feelings flow from you and affection pass to you. Sa'ad.

I didn't know how to answer, but I knew they were as sad as they were happy. Perhaps it was the attachment to the place and the people or perhaps another reason that the days would tell. I felt that my fate was eager to meet them.

The Kuwait crisis began with the invasion of the Iraqi Army on 2 August 1990. Two days later, they completely controlled Kuwait, declaring the country as one of their governorates. The occupation lasted seven months and ended with its liberation on 26 February 1991.[15]

After the crisis, my father's meeting with his friends resumed at the annex every evening. They gathered after the afternoon and evening prayers while school life returned entirely to normal. My fondness for learning was evident, as if I was repeating my mother's determination, as my father used to say. When I returned from the school, I spread my books on the floor, read what we had learnt, and did my homework regularly. This repeated scene excited my father, who asked me one day to read what was in those papers. He asked me, 'What's in this?'

---

15 Ms. Warsaw Al Sameri, this kind of narrative is called by some critics as a "stream of consciousness" and can be described briefly as a measure of continuous flow of thoughts within the human mind. The language tends to narrate the realities instead of events. I am pleased to note your use of this technique because it primarily represents your culture as a writer; there was a sense of reality present in it in a large portion and this gave it a value. You have inserted in it a lot of changes and fluctuations and temporal flow. It is a new technique in contrast to the technique of the traditional omniscient narrator. I tend to go for this type of narration, and I find it departing from the narrative context in its usual scenes of description and events and dialogue. You can replace it with a narrative event as you revise the composition of the novel. Sa'ad.

I enjoyed explaining the Arabic alphabet forms and sounds to him. He admired me when I told him these were the same alphabets in the Qur'an but that the meaning differed according to their context.[16]

He asked me, 'My dear daughter, Warsaw, can you also read a newspaper?'

I confirmed my ability to read the newspapers. I wanted to prove to myself, before anybody else, that I was Warsaw, who could surpass her peers and sisters the same way my mother did. My father used to bring me *Al Hayat*, the London newspaper, every morning. I didn't know why that paper in particular. He used to wait for me to return from school so I could read the headlines to him. He would ask me to read all the details if he liked the subject, before letting me move to another topic. My relationship with my father developed as I spent more time with him. He asked me to read the same news to his friends too. I found him proud of me and saw how surprised his friends were. They wondered how a young girl could read like grown-ups and know what they didn't know. Things went by quickly, and one of them asked me to read some poetry and another to write a line or two. My father asked them to wait until tomorrow.

My father recited some Bedouin poems that he inherited from his father and his tribe, and I quickly learnt them by heart and became familiar with the music of poetry which I knew its name later to be *Haijna*. As usual, my father's friends arrived after the evening prayer, and he asked me to

---

16 You are great here. It's beneficial to mention here the recipient's problems, as he reads far from the context, because he will divert its meanings. I wish to read what you write in your eyes soon, so the creator and the recipient meet in one context. Sa'ad.

recite a poem. He felt proud, and I grew happier when any one of them admired my ability to learn by heart and repeat. I was more attached to my father than before, and we spent more time together. With my increased confidence, my father gave me another task: to look after my brothers and ensure their punctuality in praying.

As usual, my father would get up at dawn before the prayer announcement and wake up my brothers to pray; some of them did pray but others went to bed the moment he left the house. He asked my mother to watch them but my mother grumbled loudly for she never liked screaming especially in the morning.

My father remained with his Bedouin disposition and it was hard on my brothers. His relationship with them would reach the stage of scolding when it came to delaying prayers,[17] especially dawn prayers, and if they let their beards grow without trimming. His first mission was to wake up my brothers every morning to perform prayers. It became a fright for my brothers and not a punishment by God or a desire for Heaven. He would delegate his intelligence to me when he left the house or went to the mosque. He would ask me who woke up, who prayed and who didn't. One day, I told him three of them didn't wake up, and he became outraged. He went inside and pulled them out of the bed until everything was quiet in the house. We were all scared. I said to him, 'It is because

---

17 My dear, I imagine you can cast the events in a consecutive manner so that the recipient is able to follow. I've noticed here your description of events instead of narrating them; this is considered a flaw of narration which can be overcome after revising the novel. Keep into consideration the narrative aspect and maintain the style. Sa'ad.

you are our father you scold us every moment. You tell us precisely what you want, and we will obey and comply without screaming.'

My father looked at me and my eyes were focused on his. I noticed the change in his attitude gradually from frowning to relaxing and even smiling. He didn't denounce what I said but tried to hide his smile. Soon he expressed his admiration for my eloquence and my personality and said, 'This is Warsaw, the daughter of her mother, Hessa, and Derrida, a daughter of Derrida.'

Since my childhood, I have become so close to my father. He used to take me with him on his visits to villages and Bedouin camps. We used to leave early after dawn prayers in his Hilux pickup, which he considered a treasure and was very proud of it, like all Bedouins. He carried all kinds of foods, carcasses, vegetables, and fruits. After tens of kilometres, we would distribute food to his family and relatives. He used to repeat his sentences: this is my cousin's home, my niece's, and that is my brother-in-law's, and so on. We would end those weekly tasks before the noon call for prayers, then would go to the house of my uncle, Hamdan.

I felt at home there and at my grandfather's place. Many members of the family met others at two large tables, one for men and the other for women. I got used to and became familiar with the house and its residents. I knew and built a strong relationship with them all. Once, I heard my uncle reminding my father, 'Listen, Khalaf, as we had agreed since her birth, your daughter, Warsaw, is for her cousin Butti; she has no one but her cousin who can defend her and maintain her dignity.'

My father remained obedient to my uncle all the time. That was what made him feel that he was in his own home. After lunch, he would take a siesta in the *majlis* while I played with the children, as my relationship with them developed, except with that so-called Butti. I spent a childlike time with my nephews and nieces and a long time with them, and I loved them all except Butti.

My cousins competed with each other by showing their Bedouin talents, including camel riding. The animal was distinguished by its hump and its dangling lower lip. Butti asked me to ride as he did, but I feared the camel and her mouth, particularly while she was ruminating over food. They laughed at my ignorance and fear of the camel. I felt sad about that and said, to change the subject and get rid of the embarrassment, 'Can anyone among you sail on a boat? Can anyone of you swim in the sea of Jeddah?' They replied negatively, and I acted like I was laughing at them; I ridiculed them as they did to me and I said, 'This is the difference between the Bedouins and urban dwellers; we sail a boat in the sea and ride bicycles on land, and you still ride camels, milk them, and even sleep with them.'

One night, which remained hanging in mind, was in the desert with my Bedouin cousins. I was about to fall asleep with the rest of the children near the wall, when I heard wolves howling. I ran from the wall and sought protection from my brother, Abdullah. He felt me, so we decided to stick my back to his and his to mine, so he could protect me, and I could cover him. We decided not to mention our fright to our cousins, for fear of being teased by them.

The Bedouin boys slept in the same bed, with their bodies close to each other, which generated warmth. When I reached twelve, my father asked me to keep away from those children, calling them adolescents and calling me a grown-up girl, *hurma*. My mother asked me to keep away from all males except my brothers. At that time, I didn't know why my brothers were an exception.

Later, my father agreed with my mother that I should be covered in black from the top of my head to the bottom of my feet. From then, I became a mobile black tent. He was strict regarding men, insisting that I should not greet any man, even if he had greeted me. I asked them why. My father said it was religious principles, and my mother said it was part of customs and tradition. My mother often would not agree with my father's opinion and would contradict him, and often her opinion was right.

That prohibition included all my cousins and even my brothers-in-law. That relieved me from talking to Butti. I didn't know why that decision was made, but we had to obey without further discussion. My mother said it was the life of Bedouins. A human being's life was like a single leaf on the tree of life; if he tried to separate himself from the tree's origin, he would fall. If he tried to live away from the rest of the leaves, he would be liable to be left at the mercy of the wind, worms and animals. I did not know where my mother borrowed that beautiful simile from.

Thus, the gap became broader and deeper between me and all the males but the relations between the males intensified. In contrast, women became secluded in closed societies, knowing no one except close relatives. I began to get used to this big gap imposed on both sexes and questions were not erased from my inner soul. Before adolescence, I had no chance to chat with males, and communication lines were severed, even by words or signs. Boys were left alone, and we became two social entities: a masculine group giving orders and another feminine group obeying the orders.

Those were the most important pauses of my childhood. Dr. Sa'ad, could we put all of those pauses together in a framework called a novel? Do you find these points essential to relate my tale from A to Z?[18]

---

18 I don't know which names to call you now, Warsaw or Derrida? Both aroused my curiosity to meet you and get to know you closely. As for the answer to your question, I can find these events ripe for a novel. The critical novel of society must move away from embellishment; you read the reality and dismantle all its features. And we agreed that I would be honest with you. So, I'll remind you of what one critic said: 'There's a big difference between creativity and composition. Composing is a reconfiguration of old objects in different ways, but they remain old, and creativity is a new process of creating texts.' More precisely, I may say that composition is like rearranging your home furniture; you might redo it beautifully, but you use the same piece of furniture and you don't add anything new to it, whereas creativity is to turn a chair, for example, to a bed. I expect creativity from you. Sa'ad.

6

My First Marriage Was a Delayed Consolation…

I wrote this second part, which was based on my verbal agreement with Dr. Sa'ad. That agreement was about writing chapters of my autobiography for him to review. I would then rewrite it based on his critical remarks. Then, we could see if those anecdotes were worth printing. By that time, we would call it a novel that publishers would accept for publishing, and readers would benefit from other people's experience. We would then hope that it would reach the hands of the Advisor, who deprived my son of his rights. With this collaboration with Dr. Sa'ad, serious work would be considered a duty. We would see the outcome of the cooperation, both criticism and narration in creating a genre of creative writing. Let me start now by recollecting the most critical stages of my life,[19]

---

19 It would be nice, my dear, to be familiar with this narrative technique known as flashback. It is a technique that helps you relate your novel and explain the contradictions in complex characters through explanatory expositions. It will also let you use dialogue in a dramatic form and pause to feel the emotional upsetting of the characters you lived with. Your narration began with the introduction of an event that should stop at a particular point

those where I was influenced by the environment in which I lived, and how a human does not contribute but only with a minor part of his biography.

I always recall the stage that is called the "transitional phase". I had to keep away from men except my father, brothers and uncles. They clothed me in black from the top of my head to the bottom of my toes. It was the law and a traditional requirement, and we had to live in its orbit.

I went out for the first time after the *Sharia* requirement; I was not used to the life in this black tent. I walked with my brother, Abdullah, to the open space behind our house. At that time, I still felt like a child and wanted to play as I did yesterday. I tried to take off that cloth covering the whole of my head. I asked my brother, who was two years my senior, 'Why all of this, Aboudi?'

He answered me by repeating what my father had already said, 'The legal *hijab* protects women from errors and guards them against stumbling.'

His sentence remained vague; I did not comprehend its precise meaning. What errors were they talking about? What type of *Sharia* were they looking for? My brother said a woman showing her face, palms, and hair is lecherous.

---

and take us back to the past, with narrating the past events in a progressive manner to the point of halt. It is not like the recollection technique except in freezing the motion and slowing time. I find, Warsaw, that you need to focus on the important stages in your life that we can invest in to arrive at the needed objective of this narrative experience. I found you a pioneering woman ahead of the thought of the environment. I was happy to deal with it narrative-wise. Sa'ad.

I understood nothing of the answer. I went back to my mother and asked her about that tent. She said, 'They want a woman to close her eyes and walk behind the man in the name of religion, and your tent became a must, Warsaw; nothing will be visible from you, Derrida.'

Days passed by, and I was admitted to high school. My lifestyle had changed; no men should be seen except my brothers. I would eavesdrop on any male coughing if I desired to listen to any man's voice. I would observe any man and try to find out a way to talk to him. Why should I avoid a man if he would be my future husband?

At the age of eighteen, I was enrolled at the university. I thought it would be my salvation and would take me out of the house prison. When browsing through philosophy and psychology books, I would search for reasons behind the separation of the two sexes in everything and the theoretical differences between the Arab society and its oriental equivalent.

My father came to see me in the evening, after completing my freshman year. He never hid what he had on mind. He was clear and unambivalent when discussing any subject. I would usually know his intentions before speaking. My father was like a desert, where you could see everything clearly – a straightforward Bedouin. Thus, he invited me to his *majlis*, and with the love he had offered me since childhood, he made me sit on his right side. He said, 'Warsaw, in the customs of the tribe,[20] we were used to

---

20 Mystification rises from the fact that the elders of the siblings assign their daughters and children to each other from birth, and that she is for him and vice versa. It's a lovely illustration, Warsaw. In this context, I would say that this footnote speech is one of the elements of the parallel text, which is one of the helping aids to hold the text's connotations superficially or profoundly. It is a very important

mystification, the habit that when a baby girl was born, we would name her a bride for her cousin in marriage. This is a kind of arranged marriage. You were named to your cousin Butti – an able, good, generous, magnanimous Bedouin from the village who would protect and safeguard you.'

With the same audacity that I inherited from my mother, Hessa, and the confidence I acquired from my undergraduate studies, I refused the concept of arranged marriage. Consequently, I rejected my cousin Butti, because he was weak, and he had no ambition in life. What was more important was that I had found him unpleasant since childhood.[21]

My father was angry and moved the case to my mother, who was not usually neutral and had always sided with me. She told him, 'Warsaw is the one who is getting married. Why do you force her to marry someone she doesn't want? If you fear your brother, Hamdan, my daughter is more important than your brother and his son.'

My father always kept quiet when my mother spoke sharply, defending her children. My father's silence was unnatural and imposed, not like the one which watches the events and depends on the action, not reaction. In response, he said, 'What should I say to my brother?

In turn, I interfered and said, 'Don't tell him anything; time will solve everything.'

---

threshold for accessing the narrative to capture its purposes. In my view, the footnotes are a reference and reference text which is associated with a word, sentence and even a paragraph. And you have exceeded in its use of the strange words in other societies. Sa'ad.

21 My dear Warsaw, the language in this chapter is a reporting language; it tells us about events and gives a report, but it does not list the events in detail. You should rewrite the text to show the event, description and dialogue. Sa'ad.

Relations between my father and me became calm, and no sooner had that happened than when he was affected by the diseases of old age. It started with the renal failure that required many visits to various hospitals. My father fell sick and, as a result, knew the value of his health. With sickness, he became less mobile and more lenient and tolerant. As his body gradually became frail, he became less argumentative, more cool-tempered and silence fell on him like darkness. After nearly two months, another man proposed to me. The problem, this time, was that he was an urban employee from Buraydah in Al Qassim region. I did my best to get my father to agree to that marriage. He categorically refused the idea of an urban man marrying a tribal woman.

When I failed to convince him, I went to my mother, expressing my strong desire to marry the man. She was convinced because she was an urban dweller too and knew the vast difference in dealing between an urban dweller and a tribesman Bedouin. I was thrilled but afraid my uncle might interfere with all his might.

My mother waited for the return of my father from his *majlis* after his friends had gone. She was less concerned about his health, offered him some coffee, and said, 'Your daughter, Warsaw, agreed to marry Saud.'

'How could she decide to agree to an urban dweller? I don't understand.'

'Saud is an urban dweller of Buraydah, from a well-known family and a military administrator.'

As was his habit when entering a discussion with my mother, he would keep silent and begin to revise his thoughts and rearrange them to complement what my mother said. Very soon, she had convinced him after just a few attempts. The only major obstacle was my father's fear of Uncle Hamdan, his senior brother. I accepted the suitor and refused my cousin. With her smartness, my mother hurriedly prepared for the engagement procedure that we locally call *malcha*.

A marriage couldn't remain secret, as it was meant to be public, as my father said. The news of the *malcha*, the marriage contract, reached my uncles and their sons and they were in a rage, as expected. Like a military armoured vehicle, Uncle Hamdan arrived at Al Qassim with feverish anger.

My father was suffering from diabetes then; he was so concerned about this ailment that he fell victim to another. I was assured that the fear of a disease would make you suffer from its consequences. He was affected by kidney failure while he was suffering from diabetes. That made him housebound; he only left the house in a dire emergency. My uncle arrived with his boorish son, Butti. He knocked on the door, announcing himself. Everyone was dead silent. My uncle entered my father's *majlis*, while I stepped in my mother's chamber. She ushered me to sit beside her and gently rubbed my head.

I said, 'Father is ill; I fear he might give me up to my cousin, Butti.'

Mother was afraid my father might withdraw his word and hand me to my cousin on a platter of gold. She sent my brother, Abdullah, asking father to her chamber. He came with grief, as if strangled. Mother said in a clear voice, unequivocally holding me to her breast, 'Listen, Khalaf, don't withdraw your word and let my daughter into endless problems. Warsaw refused her cousin, Butti, and chose Saud. It's all over. Full stop.'

Father reassured her that he refused his brother's demand. I rose to ask him what had happened, and he said, 'My brother asked me to call you, Warsaw.'

Silence fell heavily on the place, and Mother was concerned about her daughter, but I comforted her. She asked, 'Your brother thinks he is a man. What does he want from Warsaw?'

Father repeated what Uncle had said: 'Call me your daughter, Warsaw, right now. Let her come and see her cousin, Butti.' But Father ended the subject. 'I said to Uncle: Warsaw is a bride and sees no men, even if they were close relatives, except three months after the wedding. You know these rules. I lied to him so that Warsaw didn't have to see her uncle, and then we would be sorry.'[22]

'What did he reply?'

'Your uncle groaned in his ugly voice, saying: "If Warsaw has no interest in my son, Butti, there are young men of the tribe, her cousins; she could choose whomever she likes. They are better than the stranger, who is an insult and will never honour her."'

Father repeated the dialogue that went on between the two brothers. '"The girl is betrothed to another man. It is

---

22 Warsaw, it is not possible to write the language of your father, who is illiterate, in these words. There are three methods by which you can write this dialogue. Let's start by these examples:

My father said: "Warsaw doesn't want Butti."

Or "My father said that Warsaw doesn't want Butti."

There is another method which will give the dialogue more credibility – "My father explained that Warsaw doesn't want Butti".

You better write the dialogue after understanding the characters. Keep it simple. Then, read it in a loud voice so that it becomes real. I imagine you are now practising the dialogue as you are at the top of your femininity. Sa'ad.

too late, Hamdan, and you don't want to create scandals for your brother or his daughter. People would talk if the girl was divorced before she was wedded."'

'Your uncle replied in a loud voice, "She can take any one of her cousins."'

'I told him Warsaw was betrothed to another man, and it was all over.'

After that, I saw my uncle leaving the *majlis*, resentful, clapping his hands and saying, 'This is a condolence, not a wedding; my God, our daughter went to a stranger while her cousins were present.'

One month after the crisis of matchmaking, which had involved me since my birth, my father's condition deteriorated and he was admitted to the hospital. After one week, he went into a coma, and soon diabetes ended his life. News of his death was not shocking – it was expected. I knew then that our fear of death reflected our fear of life. Mourning was held at an adjacent mosque to our house. My uncle and cousins attended, but he declined to offer Mother condolences or even greet her.

My father died, and the wedding was postponed. It was held more than three months later. We waited for my mother to be out of mourning. We decided to have an effortless wedding. We were considering the death of my father, as well as the general family situation, particularly as related to Uncle Hamdan and his son, Butti. I had just completed my first year in college and started studying major courses at the department of psychology.

After some arrangements came the big night – the wedding night. I can never forget that. My relationship with Uncle Hamdan and his sons was severed on the big night. When Saud entered my room that night, he wanted to interact with me vulgarly, without any prelude to my femininity. However, I resisted. A woman always looks for a spiritual partner before a sexual partner. I told him we should delay going to bed, as I wanted to talk to him first so that I could love him. But whenever I pushed him towards discussing any subject, there was nothing on his mind but sexual intercourse.

I asked him, 'Could you tell me something about your childhood?'

'This is our wedding night, and you are talking about children? Leave that to God; whatever comes from Him is welcome.'

I was utterly disappointed with Saud from the first night. I talked, hoping to engage him into something to talk about. I searched for a common subject. I said, 'You are a military administrator, tell me a little about the nature of your work.'

'My good lady, we aren't on duty. Leave the work for the time when we're on the duty.'

I asked him about his ambitions in life and objectives that he wanted to fulfil, but he closed all doors to discussion. He tried hard to pull me to the marital bed. That was what happened, akin to a rape. He fulfilled what he desired. After that, estrangement between us increased, becoming deep-rooted. With the passing of time, communication between us was also severed. I decided to leave his apartment for my family's home on the fifth day of our marriage.

It was early morning and he had left home for his military duty. I was assured that happiness required struggle to be attained. I had to find a solution to that problem. I packed my things and called a cab to take me to my father's house.[23] My mother received me while preparing her breakfast, but she was shocked when she saw my suitcase. Before she started her reproach, I threw myself in her lap, with tears flowing from my eyes.

She asked, 'Warsaw, what happened?'

'I don't want him, Mum. I don't want him. I couldn't talk to him. We had nothing in common except that he wanted to take me to bed. I am a human being, Mum, not merely a bed. This is a real boor, Mum.'[24] I began to gain from my mother's kindness, who understood a female's and especially a bride's feelings. I realised the stress of sadness decreases when shared.

She said, 'Let's wait for your brother's decision and how to deal with him.'

I swore not to be married to him, even if my brothers forced me. I spent the day lamenting my luck until my brothers returned from work. Abdullah was the first to arrive. Mother told him what had happened. He asked us to be frank and to cooperate with him so we could find an answer and a solution to this sudden problem.

He asked,[25] 'What's wrong? Nothing serious, I hope.'

---

23 Warsaw, you provide important signals that need to be taken into account. Some consider that the fiction language should be sober and even classic. In my view, however, the power of fiction lies in its ability to go beyond lexical restraint. Fiction is not a static lexicon, but a moving keystone that goes along with the main characters. And that's what forces me to respect your writing. Sa'ad.

24 I find that you use what is known as the "linguistic syndrome", which is common in polyphonic narrative, used to highlight different characters and perspectives. I wring your hands, Warsaw. Sa'ad.

25 You're an expert in narrative. As we shall see, a word in the novel is based on three voices: the voice of the author, the voice of the

'I don't want him; he's trivial, stupid, a fool and a bull. I have no feelings for him. I dislike him and that is enough. I don't want him.'

Mohammed said, 'Please try to understand, sister, if a man doesn't release his sexual energy in his wife's bed, he would set it free outside it. Please consider this profoundly.'

Abdullah didn't accept those reasons, and my mother backed him on that. They were both concerned that if divorce was sought, my uncle and his sons would be rejoicing after I had refused my cousin, Butti. After many attempts, they insisted that I should return to his home and give him another chance, hoping my mood would change and my lot would improve.

I reluctantly went back to his apartment, an exhausted body without a soul. Life continued coldly between us without any taste. I sought a person with a mind, but he only desired a body. Three months later, signs of pregnancy came as a shock. I didn't wish to be pregnant. However, my mother and brother rejoiced in the hope that my feelings towards my husband, Saud, would change, but after performing my duties as a wife, I tried to satisfy him by fulfilling his marital rights and bearing my marriage responsibilities. However, my heart had a different language that rejected his presence beside me. My resentment gradually increased until I decided to leave his apartment when I was in my sixth month of pregnancy. I

---

narrator, as well as the voice of the internal dialogue or monologue. In the narrative of multiplicity of voices that we are working on now, the first and the second types are supposed to disappear successively in the interest of the third one, to add realism to contrasting points of view between characters. Well done. Sa'ad.

said to him, 'My pregnancy exhausts me, and I would like to be with my mother at her place.'

He consented as if the issue meant nothing to him. I left for my mother's home with a blown-up belly and a painful mind. I stayed there until the time of delivery and the birth of my first daughter, Swar. Saud was close to me during delivery, but my sentiments remained unchanged and rather cold. I hated him touching or speaking to me. I began to hate looking at him. I spent three months with Mum after delivery, and Saud came asking me to return to his apartment, saying, 'You must return to your home, and I need Swar to fill my life.'

I declined to return to his apartment and insisted on remaining at my mother's home just to be reassured about Swar's safety. He tried hard to make me change my mind and return to his apartment, but I asked him what my mother was afraid of. I said to him, 'Saud, divorce me.'

He didn't look in my face, but started talking to my brother, Abdullah, and left the house. My mother was enraged. She and my brothers all had a different view. They didn't discuss it with me but forced me to leave the house and return to the marital home. They said a newly born baby had to live with her parents. My brother, Abdullah, said, 'Your sentiments for your husband shall change with intimacy; remember that your daughter's rights are more important than yours.'

My brother, Mohammed, rebuked me, describing me as miserable, fighting all and swimming against the current. I have never forgotten his words. Am I really what he said?

I returned to the apartment, and we moved to a new two-storey house after some time. I began going to the university and took Swar to day nursery. I continued my studies voraciously, hoping to forget my failure in marriage. This condition lasted coldly for over two years. I wished to graduate with distinction to obtain a job. With a job, I should be financially independent. Then I should ask for divorce despite his refusal. Alas, it happened unexpectedly; I got pregnant again. The news was catastrophic, but brother Abdullah said, 'With children, you would get used to the family life, and problems between you two should disappear.'

I realised then that members of my family would take what people said more seriously than considering my happiness and psychological comfort. I was compelled to live this life and had no choice as my hands were tied in the holy matrimony. The wheel of life should turn, and I had to run with it and never stop looking at the future from a distance.

As I was waiting for the graduation ceremony, I went crazy with the second pregnancy and the beginning of another struggle. If one daughter was disrupting my divorce, how would it be if she had a brother or sister? My psychological situation deteriorated as my brothers and Mum rejoiced, chanting: the presence of the children will capture my attention, make me accept my husband, Saud, and live a happy life with him.[26]

---

26 My dear, boredom might slip into the reader through the hierarchy of your previous texts, which I'm feeling right now. But there is no harm in that because you follow what is known as a horizontal narrative. It is a narrative in which there are no discrepancies, surprises or even contradictions, because they are not texts based on imagination, nor on love, and because they ignore the rest of the elements underlying the novel. The previous sections were sporadic, but they would form a strong constructive block when the text was completed. It's a creative text that looks a lot like you. Your lifestyles

As soon as the summer passed, I had a newborn boy named Musa. I stayed after the birth at my mom's house too, but I refused to go back to the marital home; I never wanted it. What helped me to uphold my decision happened: I got a recommendation to be appointed as a lecturer at the same university, the one where I would later attend for a master's degree, which would give me material independence.

---

have manifested in the text by expressing a variety of experiences, and those who want to pick you up must collect all your parts, your failures before your successes. And only then can he read an exceptional novel by picking you up a mature fruit. I don't hide my desire to pick you up as a female who doesn't look like other females. Sa'ad.

7

The First Divorce Is a Walk on the Water

Finally, I decided to listen to my emotions, respect my mind and ignore any attention to what my mother wanted and what my brothers aspired me to be. Was it not enough that I had lost years of my life with this idiot? This man understood nothing in marriage but only pulling the bed. It was true that I had declined my cousin, Butti, but I fell into the trap of another man called Saud, the boor.

At that time, I recalled my mother's position and her insistence and stubbornness when she wanted to achieve any objective she had in mind. She wanted to complete her schooling but was afraid of my grandfather. She stopped in the second year of the intermediate stage of school. She won his satisfaction but lost herself. She wanted to enjoy listening to music and purchased a radio set ten times. That perseverance led her to acquire hours of relaxation with the music she liked. Tradition did not prohibit her from what she wanted. She insisted on divorce from her first husband after discovering his affair with that Egyptian woman. However, she listened to the call of the family and agreed to marry my father, the Bedouin. She remained an ordinary woman, only to marry, beget children, and die, no more than that. Now, she is the mother of another family, a compound family with two wives for one man. Yes, it was my mother, the woman that I knew, and I had inherited a lot from her. To be happy in this life, I must become like her, to shutter any barriers that stood between me and my happiness.

I made my decision, and all was over. I went to the court by myself to file a divorce case. I was asked for causes that may convince the judge. I briefly mentioned my husband's incompetence, poor lineage quality, and psychological and corporal harm. I knocked at the glass door of the court official. Without raising his head towards me, he stretched his hand and pointed to lay the papers and documents on the desk. He spoke without looking directly into my eyes, advising me as if repeating a tape familiar to him for ages, and began to reiterate it like a parrot. 'Honourable sister, remember that you have a son and a daughter. With your divorce, they would lose one of you. I advise you to reconsider your decision; divorce is a sin that shakes the Throne of God.'[27]

I expressed my insistence and that I had made up my mind after being assured of the impossibility of life between us. Divorce is a legal right and is undoubtedly lesser than other harms. I thought it was a magic innovation to end human suffering and at the same time the children's interest

---

[27] Oh, woman, even in your stubbornness you don't look like the others; I'll tell you what I think about the language of dialogue. That language which is called by some to be a "standard articulator", but I don't accept slang (purely) as a language in a literary dialogue. I would rather leave to the language absolute freedom to act and write itself through a creative text; it's what you do now. I can see you able to penetrate everybody, the body of a novel or something else. Sa'ad.

is above all consideration. Divorce, in my case, is the most convenient for them. Having sought refuge in Allah from the accursed Satan, he began documenting the case. After finishing the papers, he asked me, 'By the way, why is your name Warsaw?'

'Because I am the daughter of my mother, Derrida.'

The official raised his shoulders, surprised, then gave me a little piece of white paper with the following words written on it:

Case No. 1432/69 28[28]
Plaintiff: Warsaw d/o Khalaf Al Samri.

The date of the first session was one month from away.

My relationship with my brothers deteriorated during that exhausting month, especially with Abdullah and Mohammed. They all refused the idea of divorce, which they thought would leave a bad reputation for the woman and her family in the society. I pursued my freedom and others had to respect my human nature in adopting a decision until its implementation.[29] I attended the first session.

---

28 I found it, Warsaw. Your proposed title for the novel was *Victim*. In my view, the title should be *Victim 69*, considering the functions of a title. One of these functions stipulates that the title should be striking, expressive, exciting, and connected to the concept of the text and to the personality and orientation of the author, as well as to his philosophical and social tendencies. Based on these overlapping and sometimes contradictory views, I find that the title is a linguistic and formative sign and not supposed to be (totally) independent from the novel. I see you as a victim in the image of 69. Sa'ad.

29 My dear, this is a beautiful language; it's rhetorical and poetic and is based on the rarefaction of the sides of the language by removing them, which leads the text to divert from its ordinary use to its aesthetic task. Some readers are attracted by the linguistic form

The judge read the reasons for divorce and asked me to provide more explanations, examples and evidence. He asked me to go into details, even if they were minimal. Without hesitation, I verbally mentioned them as I had written them down. Then, I began explaining as if trying to narrate what had happened between us since the first night. The judge listened to all the details, nodding at times, and saying, 'God have mercy on us.' Then he adjourned the session until the defendant was present and listened to the defence lawyer.[30] During the second session, Saud's lawyer rejected the divorce case entirely. He added that he was prepared to meet all my demands and marital rights in front of the judge. For all that, he began a long series that I thought would never end. After that, I felt that I was carried on the top of a tornado, lifting me to the corridors of law courts.

As I returned home, the chain of problems began with my brothers. My tragedy with the courts continued for a long time, during which I got used to standing in front of judges who refused to grant me a divorce. In one of the sessions, I filed a plea, but the judge refused to divorce me and told me

---

as it carries the content of the text, therefore we find many writers are not writers, marketing miscellaneous tales by writing them in a simple language. But the literary ones do adhere to the use of proper language and this is what I look forward to seeing in your next work. Be a literary woman and be my beautiful world. Sa'ad.

30 The age of writing, that is a discourse, requires the availability of an instantaneous recipient but the age of fiction requires the availability of a reader, and a modern reader becomes part of the novel and now I have become part of your novel too, though I am not only a recipient. Therefore, the time for the narratee will be limited (like the judge here) but the time for the recipients or readers is open, which means my time as well as my destiny with you are open and ready. It's a beautiful text like yourself, whom I have not yet seen but can visualise. Sa'ad.

that Saud might win the case of recalcitrance if he filed one. The world blackened in my eyes and it closed all doors in my face. My psychological and physical condition worsened. Then I burst into tears upon leaving the court.

I saw Baha, the driver, curling his moustache and then he opened the back door for me. But before jumping in, a surprise awaited me; the family court bailiff stopped me by saying, 'Mrs. Warsaw, the judge sent me to you personally on the condition of having an official agreement between you. He would grant you a divorce in exchange for marrying you in a contract (*misyaar* marriage) after the end of the legal waiting. If you agree to that, I should arrange for a meeting at his office. The divorce would then be just a matter of time.'[31]

The offer fell on me like a thunderbolt. What is this bailiff saying? Did the judge send him? Or is there something secret that I should know? I asked the bailiff what if I declined the judge's offer.

He said, 'The judgement is evident, and you are a mother of two; divorce is considered a corruption in society.' The bailiff gave me his telephone number and asked me to call him if I changed my mind so he could arrange a meeting with the judge.

I clapped and bit my lips, as if to say, *If our Judge is obsessed with sex, then the disposition of all residents of the house is sex.*

---

31 My beautiful Warsaw, this is a narrative irony which you can exploit in the next of events. Here, there are some differences between realistic and imagined text. Realism forces you to tell what happened, and imagination makes the recipient captive to the text if the novelist is at their best. And that's what I wait for you to copy fairly and rewrite the text, as I wait for you to surprise me when we meet. Sa'ad.

After one week of contemplation and planning, I decided to end the doubts and resort to certainty. I called the bailiff and asked to meet the judge in his office. He asked me for some time. A call came before noon, asking me to be present after the noon prayer on Wednesday. He asked me to go directly without telling anyone due to the status of the judge and the sensitivity in the court and the kingdom in general.

I went to the bailiff at the appointed time, and he ushered me to the judge after gaining his permission. I went in and found him in a black *abaya* and his *shomagh* on his head and chest. I stared into his face and found it lacking dignity; the reverence that he had in the court had disappeared. He made me sit on the right side of his office. He took off his spectacles, placed them on the table, and kept wiping his black beard. He said, moving his index and middle finger, 'Mrs. Warsaw, you realise the difficulty of granting you a divorce, and you know the scandals that would arise because of that. As I don't want to divert from *Sharia*, I would suggest the lesser of the two evils. I would divorce you from your husband on condition of marrying you. Thus, you fulfil your wish, and I will stop the corruption in society. Well, what do you think of this demonic offer?'

I was sure of the truthfulness of the offer, agreeing to the *misyaar* marriage from the judge in exchange for getting a divorce. I was convinced that when a person allowed his tradition and customs to be established for generations, he would never develop and progress in coming generations. It is a trade in the name of religion.

I picked up my *abaya*, papers and handbag and proceeded to the door. Before leaving, I turned to him, saying, 'I shall stay in touch if there is something new or if I have made up my mind.'

I was approaching thirty. I was torn between the fire of divorce and the flames of society, and this polygamist *shaikh* added another fire. I couldn't find water to put out all these fires. I went back home to consider that offer. I reviewed all the difficulties that I went through. Eight years have elapsed since the tragedy of my marriage to Saud, and this should not pass without reaping its fruit. I was sure that laws were made to regulate society and supposed to safeguard the interests of the community, but I found that they protected the interests of the clergy.

Problems and calamities led to my marginalisation during those eight years.[32] Those coincided with the custody of the children hanging between their father and me.[33] One day, I went to fetch them from their father's house. On knocking on the door, Musa came to hug me and held my head, fearing it might be a long time before seeing me again. My tears flowed involuntarily, and I asked him to go inside, promising to see him on Thursday afternoon according to the court's decision. I left the place with Baha. I felt pain all over my body and wept bitterly when a call came from their father.

---

32 Dear Warsaw, I should like to pay tribute here to your use of the time-jumping technique that does not compromise the sequence of events. It is a technique that is commonly used in flashback, the benefits of which are to prepare the reader and halt the flow of time of events. That's what excites me to dig up your whole past and get to know you. Sa'ad.

33 Irony is defined as an unexpected end or shocking event. The judge offered you the *misyaar* marriage in exchange for your divorce; the perfect irony. I want you to write it later in a streamlined style that does not look intentional to the reader. Sa'ad.

'What do you want, you woman? Leave us alone.'

That night, I returned home, attending to my wounds while preoccupied with the judge's offer. I didn't know at the time how to invest this sudden offer with the pain of losing the children. I waited before taking any decision and postponed my attendance at the university until the beginning of the week. The days were very similar in this miserable period of my life. I noticed so many whispers and gossip among my colleagues. It was the world of women in general, and in Al Qassim in particular. I knew what they were thinking of and backbiting about what would happen when I got divorced.

I spent those nights thinking carefully of the judge's offer and his desire to obtain sex with me despite his old age. I guessed that sex to him was a desire to renew life. I began to think of the reasons and found myself applying what I learnt in psychology books. I began to talk to myself: 'Warsaw, if you find yourself unable to solve a problem, don't think of its difficulty; start working on solving it, and thoughts and deeds will arrive consecutively.'

Divorce became my obsession that haunted me in sleep and perhaps even at the time of death. Because our bodies sleep and our minds are awake, I dreamt of buying bread and was happy. I took the bread home and wanted to eat it but it turned hard and unsuitable for consumption. I tried again, but it broke into pieces in my hand. I woke up after midnight while the bread and the judge occupied an ample space in my mind. Here, I thought of how I could buy the judge's offer and keep it dry in his hands, unable to eat it. The breaking of the bread before the judge could swallow it was a good omen.

I decided to accept the judge's offer, provided I wouldn't fall into his hands to lure him, nor be easy prey to him. I went to the university in the morning and asked the section head to permit me to leave after the end of my lectures.

I left the university and went to the court. I told Baha, the driver, to remain near the gate of the court. I entered the court and saw the bailiff outside the judge's office. He recognised me and hurried towards me. He asked me by a sign of his hand to sit down on a metal chair and wait for a minute. He went into the judge's office and returned, smiling. 'Greetings, Professor Warsaw. The *shaikh* is waiting for you inside. Don't forget my sweets.'

I entered the judge's office and found him without an *abaya*, and he spread his *shomagh* on both sides of his body. He stood up, welcoming me. 'Welcome, Mrs. Warsaw. I was sure of your consent.'[34]

I smiled, and that was a smile of shame. He stood facing me and asked me to apply for an appeal, and he said he should take care of the rest of the case. I asked him if he was married. He mentioned that he had three wives. I denounced that he should think of the fourth. He said, 'Mrs. Warsaw, lightning only shines in darkness; the darker it gets, the shinier it becomes. When I set my eyes on you, I didn't desire any of my wives as I desire you.'

He asked for my telephone number. The moment I left his office, he called me. That was repeated every morning

---

34 Darling, far from the text and criticism, I don't hide my feelings to you. I've started to feel jealous here, and that's the proof of your narrative success. I was flooded over by text and I've drowned. I'm eager to see what's coming, and I want to meet you as soon as possible. Sa'ad.

and evening. Three days later, the bailiff called to tell me about the appeal date and the necessity of my presence at the court at 8am in the morning. I went there as if I was on the first Day of Judgement. I saw Saud, who preceded me to the court.

I sat with the other contestants awaiting the judgements. I was afraid to listen to the pronouncement of the judgements. I didn't know what the next stage of my life would be. The hall was full of contestants waiting for the court's decisions. The judge started by reading the names and the judgement in every case. He read, 'Case number sixty-nine. The *Sharia* Court ordained by divorcing Warsaw, daughter of Khalaf Al Samri, from her husband, Saud Abdullah Al Fehaid, due to incompatibility of lineage.'[35]

I left the court, and the bailiff told me all rulings would be ready within a fortnight but for that I was exceptional. I managed to receive the ready judgement from the opposite office – a paper with the title: *Marriage Annulment*. I didn't know how I spent eight years as I did for the sake of obtaining that paper. I had mixed feelings, and I didn't know whether to be happy with that paper or sad about the failure of my first marriage. I should proceed to the future, making my first step on the water. I felt pain as if wearing a dress of happiness.

With that paper, I obtained the freedom I was looking forward to, and I was holding it then. While looking at the ruling, I wondered what my family and social status would be as a divorced person. I was still beautiful and young, but

---

35 Warsaw, that's very appropriate. We can rely on the language imbalance, and devise what the events are intended for, to create an exciting title, as we have discussed previously. Sa'ad.

with two children! There were questions I needed a long time to understand and answer.

I left the court, and I couldn't believe what happened: for what I suffered from and failed to achieve in eight years, that judge could do it in two weeks. Outside the court, the driver was waiting for me very close to the main entrance. He bit his lower lip as if hiding something. As I left, I had a call from the bailiff.

'The *shaikh* sends his regards and tells you the divorce document will be ready in two weeks. I shall call you when it is prepared. Don't forget my sweets!'

'I already have the judgement.'

'The judge did not stamp the paper you had.'

During those two weeks, I was bombarded with love letters from the *shaikh*. He told me about an apartment registered in my name that would be for us. He also discussed a marriage present, the furniture, and other required things. He also insisted on the necessity of keeping our marriage a guarded secret. He said, 'Darling Warsaw, our marriage present is an apartment in your name. I would register it after the *Al Eddah* (waiting period). All your demands are granted.'

After two weeks, I obtained the document, on which it was written: *Annulment of Marriage Contract.*[36]

I was so happy with that paper, but something remained broken inside me. I obtained my freedom and felt like flying in the sky, but where would that infinite space take me? I didn't know, and that was what caused me endless worry. I

---

36 Dearest Warsaw, I feel pain of the situation that you are entangled in. I hope the next won't be a stab directed to the reader and me personally. Sa'ad.

returned to the university on Sunday morning. On my desk, I found a large bouquet with a card written on it. *Welcome, Professor Warsaw. Your happiness is as much as you evaluate yourself. Best wishes for a happy life. Dr. Abdul Rahman/The University Advisor.*

8

A Desire for a Positive Experiment Is a Negative State...

News of my divorce spread all over the place, though only one month had passed. Offers for marriage came from everywhere. I never felt that those men were looking for a female's heart as much as they searched for a body to satisfy their lusts. Wolves were looking for flesh to bite in the name of *misyaa*r marriage. Most of them were desiring a second wife clandestinely, all under the pretext of *Sharia* Law. But I had already decided with full satisfaction and assertion: no marriage again. For me, freedom has no cost.

After a lavish week since I had gained my freedom, the day came when Baha, the driver, as usual was waiting for me at the university parking lot. I reached him after an exhausting day. I wanted to remove some of my clothes that kept me in the unwanted heat. Nothing was visible of me except my eyes and hands. I sat in the rear seat and began to get rid of the stockings and the gloves. Contrary to his usual habit, the Asian driver turned to look at me. I rebuked him for looking. He lowered his vision and handed me a piece of white paper, saying, 'Madam, a man wearing a *shomagh* came here and gave me this.'

I took the piece of paper and found a beautiful script written on it. *Mrs. Warsaw, I wish you could call me to communicate...* Under this sentence, he placed his telephone number and his name, Mohammed. I asked the driver how this Mohammed looked like. I understood he was a young Saudi man from his attire and way of talking. I didn't care much. I took the number and put it in my handbag. I reached home, and from my room, I sent a WhatsApp message to the number. The reply came quickly, as if the man was carrying his mobile phone and waiting for me anxiously. I greeted him, and the answer came after that. *This is Mohammed from the Office of Registration at the university. I came to know that you are divorced. I want to marry you legally. All your demands are granted.*

So, this is the eye of society! And this is its language! A view and a belief that degrade a woman, as I was certain that most of our general beliefs are erroneous; these are wrong values, imaginary, destructive and continual. I said to myself, *There is no harm in trying.* I asked him if he was married and what kind of marriage he wanted.

He said, *As you wish!*[37] I explained to him that before making any decision, and without any discussion, I declined the *misyaar* marriage. If I thought of any man, I wanted only a continuous legal marriage.

---

37 Wonderful, Warsaw. I can be certain now that your narration skills have developed; the proportion of dialogue and description has decreased, and the mode of event has sped up compared to previous sections. This is what is meant by narration and its objectives. Accordingly, you are writing a dramatic novel, one which is based on events and where the characters move temporarily from the beginning to the end place without a lot of involvement. In other words, the text in your hands is filled with time on the account of place. I hope your next narrative will be based on places where we soon will certainly meet. Sa'ad.

He mentioned that he was married, and if I wasn't interested in the *misyaar*, I would have to drop my rights as a legal wife regarding housing and alimony. I ended the conversation with my emphasis that he should have the courage of accepting my 'no' answer as he had the ability to say it. As I was used to doing in the past, I blocked his number.

After that, offers from the wolves continued to arrive until my brother, Mohammed, came to me one Friday. Listening to his hesitant voice and faltering speech, I knew what was on his mind. He told me about a man called A'aedh from our tribe who wanted my hand in marriage. Mohammed spoke at length, praising him until he nearly raised him to heaven. He mentioned that he was twenty-seven, a bachelor, had never married before and worked as a military guard. His financial position was generally good; he earned nearly a thousand Riyals. He agreed to marry a divorced woman and live with her children unconditionally.

On his insistence and brotherly recommendations, I asked for an arrangement to meet the future husband. He was the family choice, since the first was my personal choice. I met A'aedh at Mohammed's home in the presence of my brother, Abdullah. I sat with him in the *majlis* under cover in what was known as the legal encounter, as happened with my mother in one of her marriages. I posed many questions, and he listened and responded with great simplicity. I realised the cultural gap between us. At that time, I was studying for a master's degree while A'aedh was a high-school leaver. I thought the idea did not suit me; however, I recalled the recommendation of my brother, Mohammed. I remembered the wolves waiting in alert outside. After not much thought, I preferred to enter another trial, hoping it would be positive and final. I accepted marrying A'aedh after that legal encounter and the brotherly blessings. I submitted my fate to God, knowing this submission was to make sentiments and an offering to God. And that was what happened.

We agreed to have a simple wedding party two months after that encounter. Some of my brothers attended this in Al Qassim, the bridegroom's mother and his brothers only came after they had left. I was not at the peak of my happiness, as the occasion required. My mind was preoccupied with my children, Swar and Musa. I wondered what their relations would be like with their stepfather, what was waiting for us from another man, and how are they with their father. After the modest party, A'aedh took me to a middle-class hotel for a three-night honeymoon.

The beginning of the evening was romantic, without any hiccups. I sat with him, wanting to know him through a simple dialogue, preparing for the pre-bed stage. He had to convince me that he was a conversant who could show his abilities and self-confidence. If the man had no confidence in himself, no woman would be convinced of him. I asked him about his specialisation at school. He curtly said literary. Then the atmosphere changed into liking and a little hand play. I thanked God for that. Then came the bed phase, with some touches on sensitive parts and quick kisses. Then A'aedh switched off the lights and carried me between his arms to the bed.[38]

A'aedh touched my parts, aroused me, and I, in turn, moved to touch his parts, one by one. A'aedh kept moving

---

38 Beyond my monetary role, your description touched me, ignited my jealousy, and this is a success for your letter. I saw the scene in front of me. Sa'ad.

my hand whenever I got closer to feeling his organ. The attempts were repeated, but he remained reticent, refusing to be touched there. I asked him to go to have a drink of water. Closer to the door, I turned on the room lights, and he covered the lower part of his body, as if hiding a secret. I was amazed, and my eyes were wide open to this dubious situation. I said to him, 'A'aedh, you won't get what you want if I don't see your private parts.'

Under the influence of desire, he removed the blanket, and I saw something akin to vitiligo and bulges in the forbidden zone. I felt disgusted and was about to vomit. I was struck by a great disappointment. I discovered that marriage was a trap set up carefully by my brothers.[39]

From that moment, I decided not to let him have me, and my body became untouchable to him. Here, reactive waves occur when one partner refuses the advancements of another. The more I pushed him away, the more he wanted me. I pushed him many times, but he was well-built, with strong arms. He took me by force to bed and tore my underwear and slapped me. His sense of fear made him express himself more violently. I closed my eyes and covered my face. He lifted my legs, and I shouted bitterly as he tried to penetrate or rape me, crying to make him stop. He paused. He kept away for a few minutes. He contemplated my suffering. I saw the glitter in his eyes, turning him into a real wolf. He regained his breath, mobilising his power, and was in a rage, repeating the trial with more force. I pushed

---

39 Glamorous Derrida of Al Qassim, I should pay tribute to the evolution of your narrative by using rhetorical images and focusing on the dysfunction of their structure. The thrill became controlling. Sa'ad.

Victim 69

him with all my might. The man was in a state of utmost fury, holding my arms above my head. He tried to rape me, then I had no weapon except that of the female, imploring and weeping with tears flowing in streams from my eyes. I begged him to leave me alone and not to ruin my soul by violating my body.[40]

I went into one corner of the room and was sure it was a snare set up by my brothers to get rid of me, championed by Mohammed, and assisted by Abdullah. I cursed them, and I started weeping. A'aedh sat on the sofa's edge and asked me why I was crying. I couldn't be open with him to avoid infuriating him more. I said, 'Whenever I remember my children, it becomes complicated to be close to you. I could not be a wife to you. Please have mercy on me and try to understand the situation.'

I cried so much, and he could not understand why. I left his room, went to the hall, and slept on the sofa for less than an hour. When dawn crept like a tortoise, I said my prayers. I went to him, kissed him on his head, and said, 'Forgive me, A'aedh. May God have mercy on your parents.'

He raised his head, looking at me without a word. I asked him to take me to my family's house, divorce me peacefully, and not repeat what my first husband did to me. He nodded in agreement. I returned to my father's home broken-hearted, carrying my bag after less than one night of marriage.

---

40 I can only pay tribute to this narrative, which enriches the description and dialogue. You put pain on the reader's table; pain teaches us what to watch out for or avoid, it's one of the roles assigned to the novelist. Bless your femininity that strengthened and expanded the narrative. Sa'ad.

My mother met me without me saying a word, took me to her bosom, and asked me, 'What's the matter with you?'

'He is not only boorish but a leper as well.'[41]

My mother called my brothers, who came quickly. They found my bag at the door. They were all angry, and Mohammed nearly slapped me, had it not been for my mother, who stopped him. She began to console me. I realized then that who comforted you in your misfortune was the one who must have endured greater misfortunes even if he was hiding them.

Mohammed retorted, 'A'aedh is a bachelor, younger than you. You are divorced and have two children; what is your aim in life? Do you want to be independent and suffice with your job and remain at home with your children? Is this all your ambition, Warsaw? Don't be an infidel who does not thank God.'

I sat beside my mother and said to them both, 'Infidelity does not realise the meaning of life, and you don't know that. Had it not been for his diseases in the pubic area, he would not marry a divorced woman with two children. Would anyone among you like to sample his wares? One of you should test it, and the other try it. If you agree, I shall return to him. The tale is over. Full stop. None of you are my guardian.' Then, I prayed against them from the bottom of

---

41 I must pay tribute here to your conversational language. You know that dialogue comes in many ways, including internal dialogue, contextual and operative. There is the language of private dialogues, that meaning of character dialogue, through which events are formed and the characters crystallise. My beauty, success stems only from work, passion, creativity and then success, and that's what you are doing. Sa'ad.

my heart, 'May God never forgive you for this practical joke; you marry me off to a leper.'

I then asked Mohammed to call A'aedh to come immediately to the house. The man accepted, but he arrived in the afternoon. My brother informed him that I did not wish to share life with him and that I demanded to be divorced. Then, he implored him to divorce me. A'aedh wasn't as much of a rascal as Saud before him. He was weak and accepted defeat in the first round. He wished me well. Two weeks later, he stood before the judge and divorced me unconditionally, without blackmail. That was what I wanted. Thank God for that.

He said, 'You're divorced.'

One month later, I was divorced officially.

9

Souls Speak One Language...

I refused my cousin, Butti, despite the prearranged marriage custom which was still in practice and deep-rooted in the tribal mentality. I asked for a divorce from my first husband, Saud, as I did not have sentiments to exchange for his. He did not have the mentality to be a link between our incompatible thoughts. After just one night, I asked for a divorce from A'aedh because it was a healthy and moral snare. And there I was suffering from the risks of the social culture that regards a divorcee as inferior and with disdain. Those views were extended to the environment, which was supposedly to be cultured, that viewed the man and the woman as equal wings of an eagle flown by the society to heaven, as they claim.

I was looking in the corridor of life for that elixir called "love", which was a hidden secret that would transform the misery of life into an eternal bliss. That love would come suddenly. I believed in coincidence and thought. The thought became a reality the moment I met him. I met him as if the secret of my life was connected to this man. Love was imprisoned inside me, and I never saw the light of the day. When I removed that mist, the Advisor was the first to see. Love is the equivalent of truth. However, nobody can see your reality unless you stop telling lies. Then, they would consider you the utopian city of the truth. I had to strip myself of all my experiences and return to my nature. Then, the Advisor discovered my source of femininity that symbolised love. Love represented righteousness. I felt my heart pulse intensify the moment I had a glimpse of him or accidentally met him. Was that the love they were talking about, Warsaw? Who was that man?

The first time we met was when I was appointed at the university with three other new lecturers. He did not speak to us at the introductory meeting. But I noticed his body spoke as a language by itself, and in the brightness of his eyes, there were endless words. I focused on all of his body when I saw his eyes observing me, revealing his shyness. Was it love, then? The one that appealed to the outlines of the body, while love was connected to the soul.

I knew that the professor was called Abdul Rahman Bin Isa, the advisor general of the university, which issued various directives that never saw the light of the day except through him. I left his office after that meeting, but he remained in my soul. I wished my estimate would be wrong and my thoughts would fail. I began to receive calls from the secretary of the Advisor, asking me to come to his office. I quickly went and saw nothing but ordinary official orders. On Thursday, he wanted me himself. I choked upon hearing his voice.

'Professor Warsaw, the office of the Advisor wants to meet you immediately.'

I quickly headed to the toilet and put all possible powders and the Arabian and French perfumes in my bag. I flew promptly to him. My heart was preceding my steps. The secretary met me, saying, 'The Advisor is waiting for you. Go in, Professor.'

I entered and he immediately stood, welcoming me. He made me sit opposite him at the meeting table. He spoke hesitatingly, asking about my first days at the university. I answered with all shyness that all was well. He then said, 'It seems you are worried or somehow embarrassed. The place is not suitable for you to feel yourself. Would you accept my invitation at a nearby coffee shop where we feel at ease?'

The question was rapid and, without knowing, I asked him when and where. The Advisor received the tacit agreement. He stood, turning around the oblong meeting table. He lifted his *shomagh* from his broad shoulders, placing it on his head expertly, and said, 'The coffee shop at Al Qassim Rollins Hotel at 6pm.'

I expressed my acceptance with a smile. I greeted him and left his office with feelings of happiness and some concern. Mixed feelings were pulling me to him. Did he see my biodata through the department of registration? Did he know I was divorced? What would he say if he knew I had two children? Many questions began to storm in my head. I asked God to do what he wanted.

The last Wednesday of my first month at the university as a lecturer arrived. My lectures normally finished at 3pm, and I would usually leave half an hour later and go directly home. I waited in the office that day, preparing for the Thursday lessons. Time passed very slowly, declining to pass by. I left the university at five and headed to the meeting place.

There, I chose a table overlooking the entrance of the hotel. I saw those arriving and leaving the lobby of the hotel. I ordered some cold orange juice to help me relax and control myself until the Advisor arrived. I focused on the entrance. I moved from the seat support, but then reclined to see who was coming. Then I felt a finger tapping on my head. I quickly looked and saw him standing behind me. Yes, it was him, holding a large bouquet of flowers. I welcomed him. He smiled at me, sitting opposite me where hotel frequenters only saw my face and the back of the Advisor.

I didn't know what to say, and he preceded me by asking, 'How are you, Professor Warsaw?' His simplicity was on top of his politeness.

I answered him with a question, 'What do you want, Your Excellency, the Advisor?'

After a long chat and many diplomatic eccentricities, as were usual during first meetings, familiarity began to take place. This encouraged him to ask for a meeting where he might be lucky enough to have some happiness, as he described it. I didn't find any justification for refusal, so he had what he desired. We agreed to meet at the same table after one WhatsApp message to fix the time. The agreement was implicit, and an apology would be sent by a direct SMS message. The deal was done, and I was about to leave but he asked me to stay. I said to myself, *Warsaw, be quiet, don't be rash.* I apologised and was the first to leave, carrying the large bouquet. I waited a few minutes in my car, and Baha placed his mobile phone next to him, sitting silently and waiting for my signal. I saw the Advisor leaving alone, and then I left.

After that meeting, which established a golden frame for a possible affair, communications continued, and so did our messages. Gradually, disclosure of personal life became a necessity. I knew he was married and had difficulty answering my calls every time. On his side, he also appreciated my position. Our meetings at the university were very formal, and nobody could suspect an affair between us. Then came a message asking for a second meeting on the following Wednesday. I began to feel that I could set aside hesitation and anxiety and sacrifice them for the sake of love.

During the second meeting, I spotted a curious question in his eyes. I understood it and said, 'As if, so far, you don't know my social and family status! Does that mean you don't know it yet?'

'I know but I would like to hear directly from you.'

I told him about my failed marriage experiences until I began to annul the thought of marriage from my head again, but he redressed me, saying, 'Mrs. Warsaw, perhaps fate abandoned you, but it has arranged this meeting between us.'

I placed my head between my two hands, but he stretched out his hand to the bottom of my chin and raised my head. I gazed into his eyes and asked in a hoarse voice, 'And what about you, Your Excellency, the Advisor?'

In a voice full of purity and confidence, he spoke without hesitation. 'All souls have one language that understands but does not hear.' Then he began to explain his thought. "I am four years your senior, Warsaw, married, and have four children and would like to be connected to you. I wish that."

I placed my hand over my head out of shock. Is it fate? I said, 'I agree with you unconditionally, except that it should be a marriage with a full contract.'

'My dear, you are from an Al Sameri family, and I am from an urban family from Buraydah. Even if we wanted to get married, your family would disagree.'

Until then, I knew that a person was not responsible for being different, but he was responsible for meeting with the other. I asked him, '*Misyaar* again? No, no, no, why not a continuous legal marriage? I don't want to be a female for bed only.'

'Whether we like it or not, *misyaar* is a legal marriage, Warsaw.'

I explicitly said, 'I mean an official legal marriage, like your first marriage, or everything is over before it starts.'

He insisted on his proposal by explaining with confidence, as if confirming an inevitable reality, that society had a peculiar and stronger power and that we had no compatibility. I came from a tribal family, while he was from an urban family. With such a marriage, my family could sue him whenever it wanted. The judge would rule a divorce because of incompatibility, and the children would also be illegal. We had agreed that one of the reasons for our backwardness was the remaining of the tribal system in control of the government. Dr. Abdul Rahman cited many examples, some of which I knew and happened to me personally. He warned against repeating faulty experiments. He confirmed that the nation was not based on nationality alone but on the jurisprudence of the family and the tribe. I told him that our weekly meetings remained as such until we could find a solution for a legal marriage based on the proclamation and agreement of both parties.

The Advisor did not give up his repeated attempts. He persisted in bringing gifts, trying to soften my mind and loosening my tongue. I still remember talking with him about the possibility of receiving a loan from the university to buy a new car. He asked, 'What kind of car would you like to buy? How much does it cost?'

'A Toyota Corolla is a small car suitable for my children and the driver.'

The next day, I received a call from the finance department asking about the possibility of offering assistance. I told them what I wanted. They said that they would provide easy loans to the staff recommended by their superiors and pay half of it over a long period. I was convinced that the Advisor was behind the assistance. I wanted to thank him for it. He said, 'Thank me by staying in touch.'

After a year and a half of persisting trials, I became sure of his true intentions. I was convinced of his goals and agreed to marry him, but I said to him, 'My dear, my heart moved for no one but you. You should know and realise that. My love for you was like a river that flowed unobstructed, not asking for the shore it was heading to, but feeling the existence of the sea. I thought you were my shore, Abdul Rahman.'[42]

He nodded and said, 'God willing. Love, my dear, is an essential human quality. For love to appear, we must clear the way for it.'

A year and a half since our first meeting, and after his prolonged love, *misyaar* was the only solution for our marriage. After that, I thought of nothing. I just wanted to heal my wounds from past experiences. I found the cure in

---

42 I discovered the secret just now! Is it reasonable to say that the text is not creative unless the writer is in love? Is adoration the secret to life? How loving you are! Sa'ad.

the lap of the Advisor. He was discreet, romantic, kind, and a distinguished expert in bed.[43]

With him, I knew the meaning of partnership in life. In him, a woman would find all she wanted from a man for her whole life. I discovered life in him as a man and I knew that the year of happiness would pass quickly, like the passing of a day. That maximum pleasure was culminated in what any woman desired from her lover. We crowned that with a sudden pregnancy. One year was sufficient to know your beloved and plant the seeds for that relationship.[44]

I had no intention of telling him of my pregnancy except when I was sure of everything. What I was longing to take place after two months. I became sure of the pause in the monthly menstruation. After taking the medical test, I was happy with the result; I hoped that our baby would be the cause of transferring the *misyaar* into a permanent legal marriage and to be publicly declared. I hoped our son's name would be Isa bin Abdul Rahman bin Isa.

I sent him an SMS message: *I want you today to come to our meeting place before joining together. There is million-dollar news waiting for you at 6pm.*

He sent me an emoji message representing a hot kiss. I set off to the same place before the appointed time, carrying with me a bouquet befitting the occasion. I wanted to celebrate the

---

43 You might be upset by the great temporal leap here as you rewrite the script, but I see that the personal novel is the one whose people move within the scope of society; it builds up the description of the place and it doesn't waste much time. This is a good temporal leap. Sa'ad.

44 Oh, you lover. Regrettably, this is a fast and reporting language; rewrite it by mentioning events but don't describe them. To avoid this, I always advise meditative writing in the narrative, away from memorialising writing. Sa'ad.

beginning of a new life together. I danced in my walk, knowing that dancing was the utmost expression of love.

I said, 'Abdul Rahman, I am pregnant.'

He suddenly stood up as if wanting to absorb a sudden matter. His eyes became red with anger. His hands shook, and his mouth dried up and solidified like a piece of wood. He then covered his *shomagh* with a mask. He placed his black sunglasses on his eyes and started leaving with these words: 'Are you sure?' I told him about the cessation of the menstrual period and the medical-test results. But he completed his speech, 'Could a woman be pregnant through telephone calls like those we had? You should look for the father of what is inside you among the many you slept with.'

The man whom I thought was a man masked himself and left. I always thought that in sex, true love was born. I discovered that sex with the experts was a big lie that was professionally practised.

That is my story, Dr. Sa'ad. I wrote it as it happened. I am waiting for your critical comment as you see it fit. I hope these tales will make a novel and will reach those who have conscience and would be qualified to be called humans.[45]

---

45 Warsaw, I really find in you seeds of creativity that can mature with more reading and practice. It was a traditional practice to put the first section of this chapter here, that is, after the section on the birth of Isa, but you moved to put it first as a prelude. It's a time transgression which suits the narrative's modernist structure. For the creator no longer composes and builds events, as much as he copies and empties them from his memory, manipulating them with time, forward and backward. Thus, previous events appeared mostly horizontal, not obstructing personalities, and not upsetting events. I am confident that together we can write Chapter 2 in a vertical narrative structure, in which the thrill is more present and enjoyable. Sa'ad.

Part Two

Dr. Sa'ad, the critic

Introduction[46]

Having read all the sections of Part One and after lengthy WhatsApp discussions, followed by numerous phone calls, I managed to get acquainted with the many facets of Warsaw's complex character, the heroic woman who was reluctant to send me her photograph or to make a video call, even once. So, I tried to visualise her in my mind. I went through the biographies of her family: mother and father, grandfather and brothers. I also learnt about her failed marriage experiences: the first, second and, finally, the *misyaar*. I learnt from her that a crisis that could not break you would make you even stronger than before; she was stronger and more persistent. Through her text, Warsaw introduced me to her environment where she grew up as a child until that decisive moment in her life. Added to that, the background of her mother, Hessa, and her father, Khalaf. Without revealing much of her inner life, she helped me, without being aware, to delve into the corridor of her character. I absorbed a lot from what constituted her personality and began to imagine her body structure as if the true words would make the reader feel the writer and

---

46 This introduction is not from the manuscript of *Victim 69*, and it is neither for printing nor for publication. Sa'ad.

make him transfer words into images and a sentence into a visualised scene.

She narrated the tales of her early childhood, and how she was brought up in not only a conservative environment, but a rigid one. She lived through various trends of thought of the generation of her maternal grandfather, who represented the spiritual power of what was known as the *Alhaya* Committee. Warsaw was influenced by the tribal and Bedouin conservative environment and its rival, the urban one.

Warsaw was under her mother's influence and inherited her decisiveness and stubbornness and never wanted to be shaken by ordinary things in life. Then, she surpassed the forbidden and smashed the shackles of rigid thoughts. Her excessive femininity allowed her to deal with the severe problems that she faced. I must admit, in this context, that I fell under her influence too. The affliction touched me, and I fell in love with her. I desired her like many other men did. The major irony was how I fell under her influence while I hadn't met her yet. Perhaps that was due to her disguised ability to narrate, which I thought was a representation of her in words. She let me enter with the simplicity of her words to the minutest details of her personality and I was able to observe her through the lens of her words. Now, I was certain that a female is more transparent if you deal with her in thought, rather than desire. She would become more confident with praise and would reveal her life from the beginning. You would be able to penetrate her once you could absorb her and consequently own her.

That absorption was beyond the ability of Saud and A'aedh, and even her maternal grandfather and her father,

Khalaf Al Samri. It was difficult for her two brothers, Abdullah and Mohammed, to understand Warsaw, so it was impossible for them to own her. She refused her heritage and did what she liked according to her vision.

But the Advisor had empowered her with his cunningness and intelligence. He lured her with his personality and handsomeness. He caught her in his trap through his ability to deal with a female and dive into her mind. I knew then that he was the only one who touched her heart and squeezed her mind. She offered him her body willingly. But the unwanted arrived unexpectedly. The unwanted came with the birth of Isa – to face life away from the lap of his parents. That incident forced her to write part of the tale while looking for a solution to her problem. Now, I was bound to write the second part to accomplish our noble mission together. I shall now write the narrative chapters, hoping the answer will pop up through its events or after publishing it in a novel form.

I emailed her an attachment of all my narrative remarks in Part One in the footnotes. I expressed my wish to read her comments on each observation. From the beginning, Warsaw wanted to know the instances of beauty in what she wrote and to focus on points of weakness, if any, so she could rewrite that.

I would honestly say she was not like many of the writers I dealt with, who sought the appreciation of others more than the pleasure of writing itself, which would be an unfair treatment of concepts. A real writer would take pleasure at the time of writing and would not care for the praise from others. And if it happened, he would accept it humbly. That was exactly what Warsaw did in Part One.

In this context, I hope the margin remarks (footnotes) did not affect her negatively. For usually, writers would be affected by an evaluation of others as mentioned above. At the same time, he would not care to improve and evaluate himself for his own sake because – being unaware – he would try to satisfy his fake self inside him – that idol present inside him that we would all call the ego. I hope Warsaw would truly perceive her ego and move on to the right path that she wished for. Then, she would realise that her ego was an unchangeable one and she would not be upset if the criticism was unfavourable of her writing or she would not be boastful if the critique was complimenting.

I attached a file of Part One in the email and listed the significant points of exchange of roles. I would write Part Two, and she would edit it for that purpose. I expected to commit some errors in defining the characters and knowing their peculiarities, locations and crises. She should not see the critic as an angel and take no notice of the censor's scissors that would come later. I hoped we would finally agree on the final version of that exceptional work before sending it to the printers without any worrying documents from the censors.

As a critic with many years of experience in this field, I would not expect, in principle, to achieve any creative success of this narrative exercise, for at the time of writing I would be tied and at the same time start from critical theories. As far as the general artistic structures are concerned, I would rule out that any creative writer would be committed to them. If he did, in that case, he would be following their predecessors. And whoever remains, I would consider him a promising follower, but not a creative writer. This is what worries me in cooperating with Warsaw when writing Part Two of her novel.

I tried to start writing while still in Bahrain but found it very difficult. To be a creative writer, you must be unconditionally a light spirit and realise that the reader and the critic would question the creative text. If you want to be a creative writer, liberate yourself from the shackles of previous writers and be in the valley of inspiration. I recalled what one critic once said, urging creative writers to move forward: 'If you were a writer and did not know what to write, just write two hundred words on anything; this should inspire you to move forward.' I tried and tried, but I failed to do what was needed.

I decided to postpone writing until I visited Al Qassim myself and moved first to all the places that Warsaw went to, like Rafhaa, Hijrat Aljabhan, the block of flats and Al Qassim Rollins Hotel. Then I had to meet the other influential characters of Part One: Warsaw herself, the Advisor, Isa, Jaza'a, Um Humood and others. Perhaps inspiration would assist me in my creative task.

I agreed with Warsaw to make that visit so she could show me around the places where the events had happened.[47] Knowing the places would, undoubtedly, help me to imagine the possibilities of recreating them. Could a critic succeed in becoming a creative novelist?[48]

---

[47] I have found this introduction sincere, full of insight and with a deep understanding of my personality. I wish you good luck in writing Chapter 2 and the following events, so that we can trace their effects and work together to turn the text into a reality. Now, I have got an important question: don't you agree with me, Doctor, that the place should be imagined instead of being visited? Warsaw.

[48] Dear, here I am commenting on your remarks after a long time and will write now to you as if you're in front of me, and I'm living with you in absolute moments. With your comment I've found you breaking into the narrative scope after you were

Finally, I would like to repeat to you, Warsaw, and hope, that you will not consider Part One, which is in your hands, as part of the intended novel. I don't think we could consider the text and the footnotes and their effects a modern or postmodern novel, nor would I believe that writing belonged to the genre of realistic novel. Therefore, I expect that you will consider some of the remarks only.

---

only sneaking into it. When talking about the place in the fiction field, we're not just talking about the typical or physical place, we're talking about the place that the novelist uses through his feelings and imagination, that he expresses with his descriptive language technique, and that's the fact of your description of those places. The place, fictionally speaking, is a linguistic and imaginary component made by high-class literary language, consisting of verbal forms, not pure stock and images. It's the ability to give fiction the image of truth. This is what gives the novel its realistic aspect. Oh dear, I see that you are empowered by your tools, able to mention real places through matching or drawing imagined places in your words. So, the physical place of the novel was not a natural place and, if I could say, your novel text created a fantasy place in true cast. I would follow this with your words and places, hoping to write what you deserve. Sa'ad.

O master, you wouldn't mind if I disagreed with you about the novelist's definition? Warsaw.

Dearest, what a question! Your disagreement with me and others makes me happy, makes your thinking always bright. As to comment on your question, I can define the novelist as a creative or a creator, while the author is the one who scoops from his memory; he links the events together. There is a big gap between authoring a novel and creating a novel. And as I said earlier, the novelist is the one who creates a novel. *Victim 69* was your first step and probably won't be the last, despite everything you've done. If you've adored writing, worked hard and strived in its field, I trust you would be a true novelist, because you have minimal writing skills in addition to the language and decency. I wish you good luck. Sa'ad.

1

The Love for the Act of Writing...

I left Manama in Bahrain via the International Airport for Al Madina Al Munawara, a route I was used to taking whenever I visited the Prophet's Mosque. This visit was different from all other religious visits. I agreed with Warsaw to pick me up from Al Madina Hotel en route between the mosque and Al Nakhalo district. I was in touch with her from my departure from Manama until I arrived at the hotel in Al Madina. The trip went very well, as if there was a hand assisting me to go through.

I arrived at the hotel exhausted. I could see the green dome from the front window and Jabal Auhud from the side window. I relaxed for a while, then went out to start my journey. I performed my evening prayers at the Prophet's Mosque and walked around in its yard. I then had dinner at Al Bukhari Restaurant adjacent to the mosque. I breathed the dry air of Al Madina and was filled by its odour. I went back to the hotel to start another first step of the writing mission that I came purposely for. I spoke with Warsaw on WhatsApp. She answered happily, as her emojis showed. I sent her the location map of the place. She called welcomingly and said she was in town. Her voice seemed slumbering and more feminine than what I was used to in Bahrain. Perhaps the site threw its shadows on our voices before our souls; there appeared hoarseness in her voice that I wasn't used to.

Twenty minutes later, Warsaw was waiting for me at the parking lot at the side of the main street directly in front of the hotel. I looked at her small car from the balcony of my room. It was the same car she mentioned earlier, a small white Corolla. Perhaps five years had passed since she purchased it. The car she bought with a loan obtained from the university through a special recommendation by the Advisor. She sat behind the steering wheel fairly attached to it; Baha, the driver, was not with her. She released him so we could be together. I addressed myself, *The tip of the raindrop is to be found alone in the Corolla.*

Only a few minutes later, the clock ticked; it was the first time I was listening to Warsaw face to face, not as I was used to on the phone or via WhatsApp. I greeted her, and she turned to me with a smile, saying, 'You have brought lights to this place, Doctor. It is our honour.'

I felt then that the place had a language that we couldn't hear but felt it. It was a dire necessity for the narration that I had embarked on. There were vague communications between us, obscure electric sparks that I continuously received. I saw Warsaw in her true nature, not as I imagined in all her details through her words or calls. I felt I had seen her before, and the unity of the place combined similarities in language above words. From that moment, the character-building process started in preparation for writing. The first mission began with her character. I smelled, and her odour torched me. The sides of her eyes hurt me whenever she turned around. She had almond eyes, and a lone dimple on the right cheek that got deeper whenever she laughed. My tongue was held when she spoke, and I nearly swallowed it. She felt my condition. She asked me about my travel destination and the hotel.

My voice became a bit hoarse, and my tongue trembled before words came out, rolling in the air. I replied, thanks to God, and all went well. I wetted my mouth with my saliva to lessen its hardness. Warsaw smiled, and her dimple deepened, asking me in an affected Egyptian dialect, 'My God, Your Excellency is so shy? Is that the shyness of the critics when they discover the truth?' Warsaw didn't know the apparent cause for my suffering. Her calls emitted sound only, but not concealed feelings; the effect of femininity does not pass through the ether but through the unity of place. Her beauty had a penetrating power, her breath had an effective control, and the place created a desire for me to absorb everything she emitted there. I wondered if that was the means by which the novelist is agitated sexually during the writing process.

At that moment, I intended to eliminate the effect of the place and its horror before it ruined me. So, I suggested we leave for an open-air restaurant to have dinner in the presence of other customers. We could revise the remarks on Part One that I emailed to her. Before writing Part Two, we could discuss the comments and agree on the next steps. I wanted to agree with her on the best way to reach the main characters so I could do what the critics call the necessity of multiple narrators and points of view.[49] They would not

---

49 Master, I did not ask anyone for their opinion of what really happened to me; people's opinions don't matter to me because

write themselves then, and I should prompt them to speak and listen to them. Those circumstances would help me solve the puzzle of the Advisor, Isa and other characters before embarking on Part Two.

Silence fell between us while she was driving her Corolla. More than half an hour had passed before she turned to the right and slowed down. We entered a parking lot, not adjacent to any buildings but surrounded by date palms. On the right, I found a green placard with the words "Family Café". She stopped the car, placed her scarf over her head, and buttoned her *abaya* that concealed her body, and then I became more curious to gaze at her body. The more things were hidden, the more they aroused our curiosity. She asked me to walk beside her. I took a deep breath and walked with her, side by side. I was forced to look in front without being able to sneak a look at her. Closeness doesn't allow you to contemplate things in full image. We reached the gate and she asked me to precede her. A waiter received us and took us to a side corner.

She relaxed in her chair and looked horizontally, checking if eyes were watching us. She pointed with her

---

they don't know my sufferings. I don't know what points of view or advantages you're talking about. I don't want anyone to write Chapter 2 but you. Warsaw.

Dear, we agreed to have Chapter 1 by your pen and Chapter 2 by me. You wrote the events as you had seen them, and I'll write what I see. Each of us writes through a point of view. We both hide behind an idea or a particular view and, through that, we convey what we intend to the reader. Therefore, we embrace the idea of a multiplicity of voices. The characters I plan to meet won't write their own account; I'll listen to them and express them. Oh… if events happen, I might, one day, adapt your point of view. Yes, if I were you, I would see by your eyes and listen by your ears. That is what I really aspire to. Time may not help us to build a one-sided text with one point of view together. Sa'ad.

thumb that all was clear. She was comfortable in her seat. She asked the Asian waiter for a *shisha* and some tea. I asked for a plain Turkish coffee, hoping my nerves would settle down.

Usually, when the wheel of events slows down, it darts from one event to another. She asked abruptly, 'If you want to help me, why don't you write the whole novel and relieve me, Doctor? You are an academic, a graduate, a critic, a specialist, and cultured. Just relieve me. Please write it the way you like. With your studies, you could take care of all the theories you've discussed.'

Warsaw went on in her revelation to emphasise the role of the educated in defending positive values and fighting against negative ones. She seemed more academic and serious for a few minutes. I listened to her while sipping my coffee and surveying her enthusiasm in the discussion. In her talk, she referred to the damages inflicted on her by accepting the *misyaar* marriage:

'You and other intellectual leaders should have a role, a stand and commitment, a human awareness to help the society in all of this.'

It had been quite some time since I heard this sweet talk and it made me happy. I wanted then to be in the shoes of that intellectual that she praised. I sat upright and pulled my spectacles to the tip of my nose when I wanted to stare at my speaker. With my glasses on, I couldn't see further than one metre. She smiled, while I was looking at her from the top of the frame; her dimple displayed itself as if inviting me to talk. I scooped up what I could remember by heart. I spoke in a voice that I intended to be heavy, 'Warsaw, you should remember that universities produce graduates; but they do not create a novelist, a philosopher, great athletes or creative actors. Never. A university makes an academic, not a creative individual; it does not invent Beethoven, Picasso, Messi or Adil Emam. Creativity is the result of an innate intelligence that touches the heart.'

Warsaw liked my talk, in which I supported those who did not possess degrees but are talented. It seemed that I had succeeded in the first step of my mission to uplift the value of your speaker while degrading yourself. You just need to show an apparent modesty, then the task of entering his world will be easy. In return, she praised my humility as a famous critic that writers fear everywhere. That was precisely what I wanted to achieve in that formative stage. The opportunity was possible to build an ideal image of the critic to be fixed in her mind. The flickers of her voice helped me with what I wanted to communicate. I deliberately wanted to set the image.

'My dear, perhaps you didn't get what I was aiming at. Millions of people all around the world have obtained doctoral degrees. Nobody read their dissertations, while millions read creative writers; we read Anton Chekov, Najib Mahfudh, Shakespeare, Al Mutanabi and others. A creative writer is more esteemed than an academician. This is how I see the reality; although I am a critic, I regard you as higher in status than myself.

Warsaw joined the discussion, which I wanted, with a few words. She raised her eyebrows, nodding many times. She became more confident in inhaling her *shisha*, and I looked at the smoke filling the place. My silence prolonged, and the silence made her say, 'You are very clever. We need no proof or evidence. Well, why do you talk to me in classical Arabic?'

I don't know why I talk in classical Arabic when the matter concerns literature. My tongue moves at one side, and the colloquial language hides itself inside me as if literature is responsible for correcting the language when it deviated. I felt it kept me more formal and would ensure that I remained an infallible critic to her. I intended to praise her intelligence. She had only to contemplate what had happened to her with the Advisor and what could become of her child, Isa; we could steer the direction of the forthcoming events in Part Two.

I would not deny that I looked away to hide the desire boiling inside me. I avoided any side talk except the events of the novel and its worries. But I found Warsaw talking excessively, sometimes elaborating to the point of chattering. She spoke to fill the hollowness she was suffering from. I understood that by her babbling, she was expressing the suppressed pain inside her. I let my white *gutra* slip on my shoulders and finished my coffee, wondering if the power of the place had a role in this nervousness. Honestly, I didn't know what changed my feelings towards Warsaw, why I felt at home – as Nezar Qabbani said: I was the only man and she was the only woman. As if I hadn't sat with the woman earlier or didn't converse with her on the phone many times.[50]

---

50 Doctor, I thought what makes the feelings overflow is to make the narration more pleasant. But I am starting to doubt that. I think you are moving in the wrong direction. However, I'll get to the bottom of your feelings eventually. And now, I wonder if the word (many times) does not give the meaning of (frequently), why repeating, then? Isn't rhetoric in abbreviation, like what you had told me in Chapter 1? Do you allow for yourself what you've forbid for others? I've found you feigned in this paragraph too. Warsaw. I wrote these comments long after reading them, and there is no harm in saying that sincerity is a necessity for the author to communicate his idea,

Darkness fell, and the corner became a small room with a door in the form of a mobile curtain, with Warsaw discarding her scarf and her thick hair hanging on her shoulders. Her chunky body became more sensational. She glowed and I was ablaze. Was that the seduction of an enchantress? She remained serene and confident, caring nothing for my condition and temperament change. I was afraid that my falling perspiration might reveal myself for her only intention was to send her message through a readable novel so that Isa would return to the custody of his parents. She wanted to disclose it as if she knew the burden of grief would be alleviated when we shared it.

As for me, woe to me for having many worries. One of those was to transfer her tales to the readers, the second was to meet the characters and to be acquainted with them and find solutions to Warsaw's tragedies or help her solve some of her problems and start writing Part Two according to our agreement. The last wish occurred recently: my desire to win her and reach her heart and dig into her secrets. This could not be attained except by entering the text of her narrative, and to her body that everyone near her dreamt of. She was a burning fire that all men wanted to be warmed by. What a woman, Warsaw; a moving beauty that prevented me from blaming those who tried to reach her or failed and stumbled.

After dinner, I wanted to listen to her narrate the actual events in the chapters that she sent me while I was in Bahrain writing the footnotes. I was betting that there would

---

and if I actually convince you by my honest writing, this will be the core of the writer's success. As for your question about adding verbal or tandem repetition, I see it as a kind of confirmation, we need it when necessary. Sa'ad.

be differences between the oral and written language of narration. I had to compare these before starting Part Two. In the former, body language hid many things, but in the latter, the letter language was difficult to question except by the inspired ones. In the first, sounds resonated from that sound, and the tongue dawdled by the sweetness of the eye and the rosiness of the cheeks. In the second, ink is spilt on the paper or a deaf electronic message with the letter in control.[51]

I wished to listen to her tale from A to Z, from her mouth as I had read it. She smiled and then sighed, confirming that when she searched for love, she ended up as a loser, and when she smelled its odour, she fell into the Advisor's snare. She did not mind talking about her tale. However, she suggested doing so while strolling on the roads of Al Qassim. She wanted to change the direction of the conversation with the change of place. She drove her white car. At that point, I recalled her private driver, Baha, the Indian whom she usually described as stupid, but she didn't move without his assistance. I thought momentarily that he could be one of the narrators or witnesses.

I asked her, 'Do you have a driving license? Where is your private driver? Where is Baha?'

'This is the product of the new era, Doctor, the openness we wanted; no more prohibited *mahram* is needed.' She smiled and added, 'They prohibited seclusion, *khelwa*, that

---

51 Here also, I don't find anyone using such expressions. Warsaw.
Miss Beauty, there is a fundamental difference between the written and spoken languages. Within spoken language, the character crystallises and shows their features through dialogues, while in a written narration, we must raise the level of the language; it is the responsibility of the language. Sa'ad.

is the man and a woman alone in public. They only allow it with an Asian driver. Then the solitude becomes legal as if the Asian is not a man.'

She talked for a long time until she dropped me back at the hotel. She asked me if I should pack to leave town in the afternoon. We shook hands, bidding farewell until we met the following day, as she wanted. I retained her hand in mine, feeling it and asking about her plans. She winked, saying by then we would talk.

That night ended with Warsaw dropping me in a sea-like place, whose shores I could not comprehend being the son of Bahrain. I spent the night reading my notes on Part One, and writing some remarks on Part Two, waiting for Warsaw to arrive. At the appointed time in the morning, she came with blooming femininity. I checked out of the hotel and put my bag in her car, and we set out. We crossed streets and narrow lanes, and then she took the highway. I asked about our destination, which she said was Al Qassim.

We drove for hours, and Warsaw revealed her inner soul without stopping, except to refuel or buy food. We drove long, and I listened to her, hoping that paying attention to her would be the first step to attaining my desired goals. She went on and on while we entered the region of Al Qassim. Soon she pulled up at a big white building. She demanded I follow her. I asked her where we were going.

'Don't ask, Doctor. You must discover everything yourself.'

I walked by her side like a peeping Tom. The wind blew up her dress, making her bodylines more apparent. I asked for God's forgiveness. I preceded her, and as I faced the building, I read the placard at the entrance: Al Qassim

Rollins Hotel. I pointed to the name and shouted, 'Oh, yes, this is the first place, the spot for romance rendezvous.'

We entered the hotel together as our shoulders nearly touched each other, and as the distance narrowed, I perspired. We passed the red carpet towards the receptionist. She requested to book a room with two separate beds for one night. The receptionist searched the computer for a suitable room and handed us the key to Room 211. I excused myself and said, 'Pardon me, but we would like to have Room 69. Is that possible?'

She raised her eyebrows and opened her mouth in surprise, understanding what was behind the request. The bell captain carried our bags to the room. Warsaw asked me to follow her to the elevator, whose door closed quickly. Her smile gradually disappeared as if the number sixty-nine had uncovered the pain that was wandering in her memory. In turn, I sensed her wound and touched her hands. It was an opportunity to come closer to her, becoming more audacious and active. I imagined the Devil entering the elevator and standing next to us, patting my shoulder and encouraging me, but for a while, however, I preferred to wait. I sighed when we reached the first floor, and the Devil opened the door ahead of us to guide us to the coffee house on the first floor.[52] I looked at the place, and Warsaw's description

---

52 Doctor, why didn't you say café like the one I used in Chapter 1? Critics follow a rule: to dissent means to be remembered. Warsaw. As I helped to preserve the characters, one of the writer's most important responsibilities is to preserve and upgrade the language. There is no harm in using a hybrid dialogue in language where the language vocabulary will be mixed in another language for various reasons, including cultural and social plurality and others like café or taxi. Sa'ad.

wasn't that bad; but the coffee house was more spacious than I imagined. The smell of Arab incense filled the place.

She asked me, 'Could you identify the table where the Advisor and I were sitting?' I looked again and pointed to one of the two tables adjacent to the glass barrier. I went to one of them, wanting to sit down, but she said, 'Your intuition failed you. That was the one, not this one. Take a seat opposite the other chair.'

I looked directly into her eyes and asked, 'The Advisor was sitting here, wasn't he?'

She turned her face away from mine, and I knew the reason for that resentment. I wanted to stare into her eyes for a few seconds so that I could invade her privacy; Warsaw didn't want me to. I preferred to keep quiet until that moment.

'Please sit down here and tell me what you feel a few minutes later.'

The waiter came to take our orders. I asked for a plain coffee, while she asked for Turkish coffee without sugar. Then she said, 'He used to sit here, exactly in your place, nothing visible except his back. He was trying assiduously, and when he attained what he wanted, and I got pregnant, he claimed no responsibility. This is how men behave, Doctor.'

I placed my hand on my chin, enacting the role of a wise critic. I said what I recalled from the books of psychology, 'Warsaw, a man once asked a philosopher, "Why do you sit every morning on this rock watching the same river?" He answered, "Because the river could never stay the same each time; the water flows." You too, my dear, are a flowing river; this place could never be the same as it was for you, and you could never be the same to it because we do change with the place every moment.'

She kept quiet, and silence was the first step in contemplation. Then she spoke slowly about the presents that the Advisor showered her with. She was thrilled with them. Now, it became evident that every gift was bait that the Advisor used to reach her heart and then spread to the rest of her body. The situation changed – in the past, through the phone calls, I was the speaker who managed the dialogue the way I desired, and Warsaw implemented what I wanted. But with the alteration of life and change of mood, I moved to be in the presence of Warsaw's femininity, a follower who never deviated from what she wanted, and I listened more to her than talked. I executed more than suggested; I became a negative recipient.

After her first sip, her mobile phone rang. Her daughter, Swar, was on the other end to tell her about Musa, her brother, and his rising temperature. She calmed down her daughter and asked her to give her brother some Panadol pills, and to always keep in touch. Then, she spoke to Musa and asked him to stay in bed until she returned. As a result, my plans changed. Warsaw suggested that we spend the night at the Rollins Hotel and return home in the morning. Then, I would catch a cab to drive me to Rafhaa, and from there to Hijrat Aljabhan where I would meet the midwife Um Humood. Without asking her why the plan had changed, she added, 'I can see you are the master of writing and can talk nicely to Um Humood and her sister, the wet nurse, if you go alone to Rafhaa and then Aljabhan. You have said that the creative writer is independent and individualist.'

I asked her, before doing that, to look round Al Qassim's most essential areas reported in Part One of the novel. I wanted to see the houses from the outside, the academic building where the Advisor worked, and all the places and characters, if possible. In other words, to examine the locations and see the features of the characters. That would help my credibility more than searching for solutions to her tragedy and her son, Isa, before writing the events. That would also help me to deal with various characters in Al Qassim, Rafhaa, and Aljabhan.

The more I listened to present Warsaw, the more I became fascinated by her. What was the thing that changed in her but left an effect on me? Even her talking about writing and its rituals became different, as if she was a professional in writing. For how did she know that one of the essential features of creative writing was to sketch out places and characters before starting writing in earnest? She was the one who consulted me about every word before putting it down on paper. Could she surpass an academic person like me in narration?

As soon as she put down her cup, she gasped, opened her eyes, raised her eyebrows, and said, 'Don't look behind you, it's him.' She got confused; blood rose to her cheeks and she began to sweat and blush.

I wanted to hug her, but her eyebrows rose, and I asked her, 'Who?'

'A surprise, Doctor. The Advisor is behind you.' Then, she placed her scarf on her face saying, 'If he doesn't confess his crime now, I shall confront him with his crime directly. A coincidence is better than a thousand appointments. After that, writing a novel or a story is unnecessary.'

Warsaw stood up and moved towards him. I turned around to observe that great event related to two main characters in *Victim 69*. She went quickly to him and touched his shoulder, shaking him. When he turned, she retreated two steps and bent, apologising to him. 'Forgive me; I am sorry. I thought you were another person.'

She returned to her seat with a red face, ashamed and confused, repeating, 'I thought it was him. Oh yes, by God.'

I began to comfort her, to ease the situation. After a long chat, I felt delight in her heart. Suddenly, she decided not to book another room and to spend the night together in Room 69, provided each of us slept in their own bed. The following day, I would catch a cab for Rafhaa where the apartment building was, and then the driver, Abu Humood, would come to take me to Aljabhan. She would also call the midwife, Um Humood, to tell her about my visit as the father of Isa, but she had to return to her two children.

We went together to Room 69, which overlooked the main street and beyond, with lots of markets and limitless desert land. She sat on the edge of the bed asking me what had urged me to help her solve her problems, to edit Part One and write Part Two, where it holds the solutions that we were looking for. I waited for a little while to arrange my ideas and words and then said, 'Warsaw, the narration should assist others the way the writer intends to, otherwise it will be ineffective.'

She sat on the edge of one of the beds as she changed my statement to the necessity that a man should help others as he helped himself. She added to that statement that sprang from my tongue, with an intention to show off my eloquence and wisdom. She added with an emphasis that my language was like that of the Advisor's eloquence and wondered if my acts were not identical to his either.

I was then held between two fires: a beautiful woman would lay beside me, the one whose overwhelming femininity I used to imagine, and I desired her. On the other hand, the fire of the mantle of literary criticism that I wear, the one that gave me the dignity of a wise man. Would I be a man practising his manhood with that woman? Or would I be an intelligent critic dealing with the reality as he would deal impartially with a literary text. Impartiality – what a dull word!

Warsaw excused herself to go to the bathroom and prepare to sleep as she had a long day ahead tomorrow. She grabbed the towel from the bed, took off her scarf and *abaya*, and her black hair fell to the middle of her back. I stared at her body's curves and her protruding, rounded hips. I placed my head between my hands and forced myself to be a critic and stay outside the narrated text without meddling in it. I closed my eyes, and there she was, tapping on my head with her index finger, saying, 'Don't go to sleep before you have a bath.'

I raised my head as she was on the way to the bathroom. I then realised that a woman's beauty is imperfect without a slim waist. Here, she is a nymph shining like a full moon. I felt dizzy then and felt my hands shivering and spreading to my knees. Symptoms that always attack me when I am captivated by beauty. I took out my laptop to write down my remarks before writing Part Two, which started forcedly, of which I might not be able to follow up its events.

After a few minutes, Warsaw came out and I switched off the laptop. She asked me what I was doing. I told her about my next steps in writing Part Two. She came close to me. The smell of the bath's cleanliness surpassed her body's odour. She became even more delicious and desirable. She sat next to me and suggested, 'Doctor, I see you are writing a solution for every character. Move the characters and the events should move with them. Thus, you could find a solution to Isa's problem. Write and then apply the solutions.'

It seemed that Warsaw believed in my abilities to write the events of Part Two that would guarantee writing a novel and would let us know the end to Isa's problem. She saw what I wrote was viable. She spoke highly of all my comments in Part One. She confirmed her wish to take those comments and suggestions seriously and implement them as much as possible while rewriting the text. She was ready to arrange the forthcoming events and for me to visit places and meet people. Thus, I could imagine possibilities and make solutions for Isa's usurped rights. I said I should begin writing Part Two and force the Advisor to correct his error and recognise Isa. I hoped the boy would return to his parents, but I wouldn't know if I could convert the text into a reality as I had converted the reality into a text.

Warsaw went to bed wearing dark blue pyjamas and trying to conceal what she could of her charms. I tried to retain the same pure and immaculate soul of a critic. It worked according to literary and cultural frameworks, which could only have a complete text that thoroughly presented its message to humanity.

I came out of the bathroom after I had changed into my night dress. I slowly opened the door and found Warsaw deep asleep. With her back to the wall, she had placed her palm between the pillow and her right cheek. I sat on my bed reflecting on her lines and imagining some prominent people she mentioned in Part One. In her features, I saw her mother, Hessa, who asked for a divorce so she wouldn't be the second wife. I also saw some of Isa, his mother's and grandmother's stubbornness deeply rooted in him. As I looked carefully at her face, the characters became crystal clear. I took out the laptop again, drew a table and keyed in the main characters, and started writing their descriptions as they appeared in Part One and should be in Part Two's imagination.

I started to document Warsaw's description. I raised my head, looking at her sleeping in bed. I didn't find that allurement and fascination in her. I wrote, *Why do I see you now a quiet, lifeless text, except for the beauty of your body, and a language which was once affluent in your tales? When you are awake and peevish, you will bloom with life, and I find in you a more exciting and lively text. You are as if you are a volcano; if erupted, its language turns into lava, and if it sleeps, its language becomes cold stones.'*

A few minutes later, I finished typing. I turned off the laptop and switched off the room light. The only light remaining was seeping through the curtain behind Warsaw. Her body curves were deadly. I tried to resist, but I could not. I went to where she was fast asleep. I wiped her body plateau down to her waist valley. I left my lips on her dimple and kissed her cheek. I pulled the blanket over her from her feet to her neck. I was then sure of my ability to narrate the following text after having touched the characters and prepared myself for the next creative step. When would I penetrate the world of the characters, live it as if they do themselves, impersonate them to the point of assimilation? To caress the text is the first step before the penetration.

I returned to my bed and turned back to Warsaw. My heart was still hanging onto her, and my mind was searching for an excuse to relieve me of the pangs of my conscience.

2

Plotting Is Another Method of Organising Events but According to Causes...

It was now early morning. Warsaw spoke to her son, Musa, and became reassured and hopeful of his health. Then we left the hotel and she put her veil on her face, where only her eyes were visible, and then the cover turned into a *niqab*. I sat next to her as she drove, suddenly speeding up. She wasn't that experienced a driver but familiar with most of the alleys and roads. She tried to appear as an expert in her driving, speeding sometimes and overtaking cars at other times, describing some drivers as "stupid" and refusing to drive her Corolla in the first lane, not wanting others to see her as a beginner or marginal. I wondered if the situation had become ordinary and official when driving with a stranger without a *mahram*.

She said, confirming what she had said earlier, 'We've told you, Doctor, that the new era is that of opening; aren't you more honourable than the Asian driver? Why should the Asian be one of the *mahram* and you are not? Is this not a social contradiction?'

I imagined Baha's situation with her as he accompanied her when she left the house. He was silent in her presence and was happy to sneak some looks. I then kept quiet, listening to the one who was listening to me a few weeks ago. She said, while giggling, 'Silence of the critic is a speech.'

She was not worried as we approached the usual police checkpoint. Only two men were on duty while the rest remained in their car waiting for contraventions. Warsaw showed some audacity and confidence in dealing with the security men. Such nerve had an effect on the security men and they let us pass without questioning, as if audacity was a narrative message that does not need words. I asked about the wonderful qualities that she possessed to act all of this. She answered with shocking confidence, 'It's not necessary to possess wonderful qualities but you must learn how to manage these.'

Warsaw did not stop talking while I was sneaking a look upon her charms whenever she wasn't aware. I examined her excessive femininity, the one that calmed down when she went to sleep, and the one which the judge and his staff desired and her faculty colleagues, relatives and neighbours all were avaricious of. Did they all desire her body, or would they instead exploit her social status after divorce, or did they find that an outstanding quality?[53]

She told me of her wish to return quickly to her children and that she was leaving her car and the driver at my disposal. Baha would drive me to Rafhaa and other places. She parked the car in one of the taxi ranks, and there came

---

53 Doctor, will this be included in Chapter 2? Have you become now a character in the novel? I cannot believe you are in love with me! I think you only add a thrill to the text, nothing more. Warsaw.

So far, I have not been able to answer, I apologise to you and to the kind reader. Sa'ad.

Victim 69

the Indian driver with his broad moustache. She confirmed that she would stay in touch and would inform the midwife, Um Humood, to send her husband to drive me from Rafhaa to Aljabhan. She confirmed that she couldn't introduce me to them as anyone but Isa's father and that I was abroad due to some circumstances and now would wish to find a settlement for Isa's matters.

I liked having her car and the driver at my disposal. Thus, details of Part Two would be closer to reality and I could write about forthcoming events through it. She told Baha what he should do. On bidding Warsaw farewell, I kissed her forehead while her eyes flooded with tears. She included me in her prayers and said I would be the cause of her reuniting with her son, Isa. Then, without further ado, Baha set out to take me to Rafhaa.

At last, I was alone with a secondary character from Part One that may become a major one in Part Two. With Baha, I began actual writing. First, I asked him to take me to the building where Warsaw was staying before going to Hijrat Aljabhan.

I began to observe the route and recalled the descriptive narration provided by Warsaw in Part One and to find out the extent of the ability of her words to correspond with the visible reality. Is, therefore, what our eyes observe the reality itself, or is the eye and the other senses deceptive? I should search that in my own experience and Warsaw's narrative experience.

For approximately seven hours, I tried to talk to Baha, but he was close-mouthed and only answered with one or two words. I found great difficulty in communicating with him, as if he kept a secret that he didn't want to disclose, even with one word. He drove me on paved and unpaved routes. I imagined Warsaw sitting in the back seat with this driver with a thick black moustache and oily hair that was kept unshaken against the air. Warsaw would stay silent, sleeping and waking up in the back seat; did he ever sneak a peek at her? Did he desire her secretly? It didn't matter then. His role was marginal, and I didn't know if that would change in Part Two.

We reached the apartment building in Rafhaa, a middle-aged construction with apparent signs of wear over time. I called Warsaw, asking her about the room number she had occupied earlier, and she confirmed that it was twenty-two. Its rate was three hundred Riyals per night. She warned me to be cautious with the Yemeni receptionist and his Bengali assistant and not to forget to call Um Humood soon.

I carried my valise and asked Baha to look for a place for the night with any of his acquaintances until I called him. He looked at me silently, and I read many questions and some vague answers. I said to him, knowing that he wouldn't understand me, 'Baha, you couldn't come with me. I must stick to the plan and call you when necessary.'

He soon left the parking lot, leaving the dust and a vacancy that I must now fill with my presence, watch the place with my own eyes and then put down the notes. No one came to help me carry the suitcase as is customary in hotels; a sign that the building only housed those angered and the lost. I crossed the aluminium door and met the clerk who greeted me from behind his desk, and I returned his greeting. He asked me how many nights I would spend in their hospitality. The man seemed to be a Yemeni national through his accent and his *qahfiya*.

Victim 69

'One night, or perhaps more. How much will that be?'
'One night is at a 150 and two nights at 250.'
'Two nights at 200, and I want Room 22, old chap.'[54]

The man agreed to my rate. That was the first discrepancy I found in what Warsaw mentioned, perhaps the Yemeni man took advantage of her exhaustion and inability to find another place.[55] He exploited her need and dictated his own terms.

I took my small suitcase to my room, which had a small window covered with a brown bent curtain to the right and a double bed with only its four brass poles apparent. The bathroom door would open voluntarily as I tried to close it.

I felt exhausted due to the length of the route. I laid down on the bed with an old mattress. I thought it was infested with bugs, so I spread my white towel on it. I tried to relax without thinking of the reality of the past or envisaging the future, but to retain my present energy only. I was able to do that; I fell asleep very soon and woke up energetic four hours

---

54 Dear Dr. Sa'ad, why didn't you mention the dates of events as you highlighted their places? I think the date will show the goal of the novel to the Advisor. Warsaw.

My dearest, we struggle to reach the novel to the reader in general, therefore it should not be restricted by time. Since this novel is personal, and its characters move in the circle of a society, it should be based on describing the place and not focusing too much on time. Sa'ad.

55 Why did the price of the room change, Doctor? The Yemeni seems to have exploited my loneliness and my need for the room. It seems the structure of Chapter 2 will be changed based on changing data. Warsaw.

§It's a smart gesture from you, Warsaw. This is another piece of evidence that refutes the theory of the overall construction of the novel in terms of its characters and events. Here, it is true to state that a novelist begins his work alone and the characters complete it. Sa'ad.

later. After that, I called Um Humood, who answered in a hoarse, nearly akin to a masculine, voice. I said, '*Asalaam Alykum*, I am Isa's father, as his mother, Warsaw, mentioned. I'm his father, but I couldn't take the boy with me for various reasons. I hope things will change in the future, and I shall take him for a few days and bring him back until he accepts the situation.'

'Yes, this is exactly what Um Isa said. You're welcome. I shall arrange that with Isa; may God make easy your path.'

'Um Humood, please send me the same car that brought Warsaw from town and the same driver.'

She answered welcomingly. I had to wait more than two hours, as Warsaw mentioned in her description of the route from Rafhaa to Aljabhan. I could then relax and have a little nap. Could I do that, unlike what Warsaw did while she was in labour?

I left the bed and began inspecting the room again, and the toilet. I touched everything there and smelled every corner until some of Warsaw's odour was stuck on me, and her breeze blew from the pillow she laid on. So, she was here then! What were her feelings and movements like? I imagined everything in the room. I envisaged her actions and the labour pains and the combination of blood and pain.

After I had spent three hours writing down my remarks, the Yemeni receptionist knocked on my door to tell me that a man was waiting for me at the reception area. I hurried down and saw the Hilux owner, not as I exactly imagined him. He greeted me and I reciprocated with the same. He dryly asked, 'Are you Dr. Sa'ad, who is waiting for me to drive him to Um Humood in Hijrat Aljabhan?'

Victim 69

I answered affirmatively and he invited me to accompany him to his Hilux pickup. I sat next to him, recalling Warsaw's description concerning the man, his vehicle, and the route. I was expecting that he would change the switchback road, as two men wouldn't be concerned with the checkpoint on the main road, but he didn't. I saw the route and the buildings as described by Warsaw. Her description of the place was accurate, but not of a human being. How did the older man turn out to be with me? He began chatting like a tourist guide, describing the whole area, boasting of his knowledge of everything there. He even spoke about Um Humood and her relation to her sister, Um Rabi'a. I imagined for moments a vague and strong connection that related Warsaw to these two ladies. I didn't know the extent of its effect on plotting events in Part Two.

At last, we reached Hijrat Aljabhan. I saw the scattered brown houses and some Bedouin tents. Most of the latter were in black, and some in white, turning brown with the passing of time. Animal sheds surrounded the homes and several camel ponds. The driver stopped in front of an old house. He asked me to get off. I quickly asked him, 'Is this Um Humood's house?'

He answered that it was his and his wife's, Um Humood's, house. As for the house in which Um Humood worked, it was not possible to enter because it was a small women's hospital and men were not welcome. However, he would inform her of my arrival. I asked him to bring Isa and the wet nurse, Um Rabi'a, with him. Would I be able to see the child? Would he be like what Warsaw hoped for? Or did the wet nurse's milk have a different role than the mother's? Was the child's character influenced by his parents or the environment where he grew up? It was the difference between the centre and the atmosphere. Isa was the seed, the centre that grew and ramified using thousands of elements of soil, air and water, and the outer frame would be composed. I would find answers to many questions while the others would remain vague. I would have hoped to write the end of this novel after finding solutions to all its problems.

In her description of the driver, Warsaw wrote that he was silent, speaking a few words. But I found him a chatterbox who could not keep a secret, as if the distance was short between his ears and tongue. The skinny driver left me and returned accompanied by Um Humood, that Bedouin woman, a few hours later. With a stern and dry face, she was distinguished by the green tattooed dot on her chin.

I knew her from Warsaw's description before she introduced herself. She did not show any smile; she was brief in her words, as if she was wary of what was coming. She asked, 'Are you Warsaw's husband?'

I looked into her eyes and soon turned away, fearing she would discover the truth. I said, 'Yes, I was her husband and would like to have Isa for a couple of days to prepare him psychologically and return him until things are settled between me and his mother, Warsaw. Then I shall have an identity card in my name, and he will live with us as Warsaw wished.'

The woman was delighted, and I asked for her help to facilitate the matters with Isa by accepting me and agreeing to accompany me without telling him the truth that we wanted to keep it uncovered so far. She said we needed the assistance of her sister, Um Rabi'a, the woman who nursed him until he was two.

As described by Warsaw, a sturdy, heavy-moving, dark woman appeared with a child of about four or five years of age with shaggy hair, as if it was cut at home in a hurry. I looked at his brown eyes, and soon he pulled down his yellow shirt and put his hands in his brown trousers pockets. Um Humood asked him to shake hands with me, but he declined and stuck to her. He looked at Um Rabi'a, who nodded to urge him, and he hesitantly shook my hand. I told him I was a relative and had just returned from travelling. I gave him some sweets; he took them hesitantly and then backed off. I explained that I wanted to buy him some clothes, and he fell silent as he listened.

Um Humood urged her sister to help him, 'Jaza'a, you explained the issue to Isa. Don't be worried about him.'

Um Rabi'a's real name shocked me, as used by the midwife. Silence fell on me like darkness. I thought I had read this name in Part One. I must go back to read it with some concentration. There was something I couldn't understand. The driver tapped on my shoulder, turning me back to that odd scene. I found the child confused and deprived of will, not knowing what was going on around him, like a creature moved only by living instinct. I touched his head, wiped his forelock, and pulled him closer. I took out another piece of candy and gave it to him. He looked at Um Humood, who approved it. I said to him, 'Let us go to the car with Abu Humood.'

Again, he begged approval from those present. Um Humood gave me an identity card. I took it and we followed Abu Humood. Isa and I sat in the back seat and left the talkative driver alone in the front. Isa's eyes were hung on Um Humood and Um Rabi'a through the rear glass. They waved farewell to him and we moved to another chapter of the novel. I began to play with Isa in the role agreed, of that of the kind father, until the time came to deliver him to his mother. Would the writer play the part of the critic skilfully to the end? Or would Isa and fate have a different view?

The driver took us to the same apartment building. I said goodbye to the man while Isa remained hanging onto his clothes. The man comforted him and assured him that he would be back tomorrow. While he was on his way to his car, Isa's eyes were full of tears. I patted him on his shoulder and stroked his head as orphans are often treated. I took him to my room and offered him another piece of candy and some toys that perhaps he had not seen. I asked him, 'Do you know my name?' He shook his head negatively. And I said, 'I'm your father, Sa'ad. I was travelling and returned to Saudi Arabia a week ago. You're going to spend a few days with me. You will choose to live with your grandmother, Um Humood, or with me. Your mother and I are separated now. What matters to us is your happiness. The choice is yours if you want to stay with me or return to her. Now, what would you like to have for lunch?'

It was the first time hearing his voice when he said, '*Kabsat laham*.' After that, I found an empty space of love within him, waiting for me to fill it up.

I called Baha and told him to come quickly to take us back to Al Qassim as soon as possible. Many questions struck my mind: should I introduce Isa to his mother, Warsaw, or his father, the Advisor, and how to introduce him to them or introduce them to him? At that moment, I didn't know what I wanted exactly. To draw up a plan or an event to write a novel is subject to change at any time. Eight hours later, I returned to Al Qassim Rollins Hotel. I took out the ID card and saw the name of Humood on it. It was that of the son of the midwife Um Humood and I had to return it with Isa. I asked the receptionist to book me Room 69 for three days, which I might extend. After relaxing, I helped Isa take a bath and put on new clothes. Baha took us to Al Hasson Shopping Mall. I left Baha in the car. I bought some toys and clothes for Isa. I played around with him a lot until I created an air of intimacy. With time, Isa began to smile and gradually talk. It was not easy to deal with the child at the initial stage, but in the end, it was more beautiful where spontaneity governed the child's language and he expressed his feelings, and you could delve into his depths.

I spent two nights with Isa, which wasn't enough to thaw the ice and create intimacy between us. That was my first aim in this part of the novel that I could not fulfil. They were two difficult nights with a child of no identity. I knew nothing of his past except what Warsaw had said and what Um Humood and her husband offered. But why didn't have Um Rabi'a any role until now? Why was she gloomy faced? Was there another surprise in the box?

I went back to my laptop and reread Part One, where I found the name of Jaza'a during the liberation of Kuwait. I hadn't seen the two ladies yet; the real knowledge lies in the heart. I guessed it was a question of the similarity of names. I ruled out that Jaza'a was one of the girls who spent some nights in Warsaw's room. If they were them, why did Warsaw not recognise them? Was that period long enough to wipe them off her memory?

After two nights, Isa wore me out by being with me, and the arduous beginning in writing Part Two exhausted me as well. I had to fight for Isa's life because life is a precious treasure that we do not realise its value until it is wasted, then we begin to gather what we have wasted. I decided to take Isa back to Hijrat Aljabhan. Baha set off and I made good use of the time during the drive. I gave Isa lots of toys every time we made a stop at a station. I promised him that I would go to the nearest hotel to do some business and return it to him. Baha drove us to Aljabhan; Isa fixed his looks on me, then he turned aside to leave. Um Humood and her children received him, rushing towards the sweets and toys. I asked Um Humood to keep the clothes for Isa alone. I told her I would return after a day or two, hoping that pending issues with Warsaw would be settled, and then Isa would return to the bosom of his parents.

She said, 'Wait a minute, Jaza'a wants to see you.'

Um Rabi'a arrived, looking at me from top to bottom. She gazed into my eyes and said with a dry voice, 'I have not seen you before.'

'You are in Aljabhan and I am in Al Qassim.'

She was surprised about my non-Qassimi dialect. I explained to her that I had been travelling outside Saudi Arabia for a long time and that would change dialects and even languages.[56]

---

56 Doctor, I find you lying here. Is that necessary to build a narrative plot? Warsaw.
Warsaw, the plot of the real-life novel is easy to narrate. The novelist has only to organise the events of the characters in a place and time. It involves the narration organisation of the events according to their chronological sequence. But the narrative plot is where the novelist organises events according to the principle of causation, and this is what we do here for the bright future of Isa. Sa'ad.

Victim 69

After that, I left Aljabhan for Al Qassim Rollins Hotel, which I got used to, and the staff got used to me as well. I planned to spend two nights and return directly to Isa. I had a plan in my mind to arrange a meeting with the Advisor. Could this wish be fulfilled? Would I be able to add another part worthy of being included in the novel? I was sure then that the most beautiful achievements were those that remained incomplete.

3

The Illusion of Truth Is a Component of a Successful Novel...

After returning to my room at Al Qassim Rollins Hotel, where I spent two nights rereading Part One with high concentration and adding more remarks to the footnotes, I came closer and closer to the places to understand the primary and secondary characters thoroughly. I found that Warsaw's text was not rational but rather an emotional one perceived only by taste and the effects it leaves behind. Warsaw chose the structure of Part One unconsciously to be modernist and was based on description. She depended on tossing the scenes in the text as if she was narrating miscellaneous anecdotes that would form an accomplished structure. She gathered several marginal tales and created a comprehensive text with a multitude of heroes sharing heroic roles. As for me, I would choose the traditional method of building Part Two depending on the succession of time and related events.

Warsaw recorded the events of Part One as she witnessed them, inserted her own points of view into all events and without separating herself from the text; I could see her clearly in the text, *Victim 69*.[57] The thought of finding a technique for Part Two exhausted me. I placed my head on the pillow, trying to draw the means and ideas I would apply in writing Part Two, hoping to convert it into a reality what would relieve Warsaw and her son of their tragic situation, and help me end this novel that I might be trapped in by Warsaw herself.

I woke up at 8am and began working after I had had my breakfast. Google helped me find the telephone number for Al Qassim university. I called its exchange and asked for the office of the Advisor, Abdul Rahman bin Isa. I decided to use the Bahraini dialect and introduce myself in my official capacity. A female voice answered in a formal, professional manner. 'Office of the Advisor, how can I help you?'

'I am Dr. Sa'ad, a literary critic from Bahrain. I wonder if I could meet Dr. Abdul Rahman to discuss aspects of cooperation in the literary area within the university.'

The secretary asked for my phone number and promised to tell the Advisor before putting me on his schedule and

---

[57] Is this text not supposed to be a realistic narrative? I wanted to convey my tragedy to the reader, and I didn't find a method of writing other than a direct one, in which others were involved. Warsaw.

Beautiful Warsaw, I can confirm what the critics say in this regard: the further the writer is from the text, the closer the text becomes to the reality and more. To be clearer, and to help you in rewriting Chapter 1, I say: the narrative text is formulated in relation to two narrative formats. The first one is established by the narrative self and is built according to the vision of the narrator, and the one that represents the intellectual and technical components of the text itself. It's fine if you divert your vision as a narrator behind the technical components of the text. It may be a complex creative process, but it pushes the text to reach the largest possible number of readers. Sa'ad.

would come back to me in any case. Since that morning, I did not part with my mobile phone, even in the bathroom.

It was evening and the promised response never came. I began to lose hope and thought of a more helpful way, such as visiting the office of the Advisor personally. I decided to be late on Isa and wait three days before making the next move because of my honest interest in reaching the truth. The call came the following morning. The secretary's voice sounded like an official, automatic tone that she had perfectly applied. 'Dr. Sa'ad, good morning. You could visit the Advisor, Dr. Abdul Rahman, at 1pm this afternoon for half an hour. Please be brief and stick to the time.'

I was in a haste to receive this call, so when it arrived anxiety seeped through me. Why didn't Warsaw send me a photo of the Advisor? Why did she refuse to offer me a description like the other characters in Part One? Why do women prefer to conceal what they love? Was there something that Warsaw was hiding from me or both? I hope I will not fall into the trap known as a woman's snare.

I was at the Advisor's office half an hour before the appointed time. The secretary asked me to go to the waiting room, where there was only one man, and there were chairs lined up and separated by vases of artificial pots. Half an hour later, an Asian office boy ushered me to the Advisor's office. I greeted the secretary, who took me to another room with a placard saying, "Conference Room". I sat alone, scrutinising it closely. A handsome man entered the room; he was in his mid-forties, full-faced and bodied and red-cheeked. He greeted me with a loud voice. One of his eyebrows was lowered when he spoke. I thought he looked like George

Qardahi. He asked me, while shaking my hand, which made me think that he was winking at me, 'Are you Dr. Sa'ad, who asked to see me? The secretary said you are from Bahrain. Welcome, Doctor. How could I help you?'

Introducing myself, I said, 'I am from the Faculty of Arts of the University of Bahrain. We are looking for a means of cooperation with your university regarding literary talents. I can introduce some of our creative experiments and would like to be introduced to your exchange experiments.'

His right eyebrow lowered again as he agreed and promised to refer my request to the people concerned at the Faculty of Arts. Here, I expressed my consent with the idea but also showed my interest to be acquainted with the Advisor's literary side as a man with a long history in literature. I didn't want to lose the opportunity of coming closer to him to learn more about him. I confirmed my desire to acquire his literary works and benefit from his creative experiment. He welcomed the idea but suggested that this would be after working hours and outside the university campus because of his commitments and official responsibilities. He indicated that the next meeting would be next Saturday and I had to choose the place. I said, 'If that suits you, the café at Al Qassim Rollins Hotel, where I am staying.'

I was expecting his right eyebrow to lower down while speaking, but his brows rose with his silence and surprise. He suddenly stood up and left his leather seat. He went to the window, looking into the distance, distracted. Then, someone knocked at the door. The secretary came in carrying a box of Cuban luxury cigars. She left and he opened the box, took out one cigar and began puffing its smoke. He remained silent and I closely observed him. Signs of prestige and wealth were evident on him as he filled his chair, placing one leg over the other while smoking; wealthiness has its language that reveals its people. I began searching for a way to get to know him better and get closer to him. I have always read that most wealthy people are not happy. They say that most of them have a conflict with their ego, trying to satisfy it by hoarding money, prestige, and power. Usually, they are unable to fulfil it. The only exception is the generous rich, the happy one whose egos bow. I found these phrases hollow and trifle to be applied to the wealth of this man. Prestige placed him at the beginning and end of any discussion. He remained silent: was that because of his memory that I deliberately inflamed, or because of his wealth, which I expected.

I excused myself, reminding him of our meeting next Saturday. He nodded in agreement and I left with a smile. I had to collect Isa, bring him on Friday and fix an appointment for him with the Advisor that would befit the occasion. I wanted to observe them meeting by accident. Here, we would see the emotions of parenthood. Was it intuitive or social? Was it innate or acquired?

I left the university and asked Baha to take me to Aljabhan to fetch Isa half an hour before the appointed time. Baha arrived with his moustache growing darker and his hair more brilliant. He set off serving me according to the orders given to him by Warsaw.

I called Warsaw to tell her what I had written in Part Two, and I was in the process of transforming the text into reality. She was thrilled and wished me good luck. We set off, as I got used to the road and became more familiar with it.

Victim 69

I called Harayeb, telling her to prepare Isa. We finally arrived in less than the usual time. I found the boy with Harayeb and Jaza'a, dressed in new clothes and looking handsome, but the colours were inconsistent, then I recalled Warsaw's description of the two ladies. I tried to imagine what they looked like twenty years ago or more. It seemed they were the same, if my intuition was correct, as there was another matter in this story, a matter that will be looked by the critics as an irony while the readers would find it a mere coincidence.

I ended my imaginary dialogue as I showed my interest to take Isa with me. Harayeb (Um Humood) took out the ID card of her son, Humood, and passed it on to me while I focused on the green tattoo dot on her chin. We rode with Baha, heading to Al Qassim. It is preferable here to pause and not to mention what occurred between me and Isa – because you, Warsaw, want to know what would happen with the Advisor in the presence of Isa himself.

The promised Saturday arrived. I was waiting for the Advisor at the hotel's café.[58] I didn't sit at the same place where he used to sit, lest I aroused suspicions, and let the events of the novel flow as I planned. He was not very late. He was dressed in the same attire that Warsaw mentioned in Part One. Warsaw was good at describing the way of wearing his *shomagh* and the manner of his speech.

At last, I met Advisor Abdul Rahman at the same café. He came carrying some of his publications, including novels

---

58 Doctor, why do you insist on mentioning the same place? Rollins hotel café, for example. Repetition is boring. Warsaw.
Dear, the name of the place in the novel is one of the famous techniques, which leads to the construction of the text; the place sticks in the mind of the recipient by repeating it. Sa'ad.

and critical works. I looked at them as I asked him for an autograph on each book. He relaxed in his chair. I asked him about his first book, his motives for writing, and other questions to which Warsaw didn't want to know his answers. His answers were routine ones, which most writers use to leave behind something ambiguous in their personalities that might arouse doubts and curiosity.

I ordered him Turkish coffee like the one I preferred. He was excited and asked me how I knew his interest in Turkish coffee. I said to him that I had noticed the cups in his office, and he praised that, smiling at my power of observation.

I informed him I wanted to be rest assured about my son, Isa, on the sixth floor, so I excused myself and he welcomed the idea. Five minutes later, I returned with Isa Abdul Rahman bin Isa.

The child remained walking beside me while I was fully awake about any spontaneous move by either side. I wanted to register in my memory even a possible eye wink, the change of the voice tone and even the tremble of the hand etc. What a dramatic scene it was, worthy of accurate recording. Such moments could never be repeated.

I shall always recall this meeting and prepare for another one that would unite Warsaw and Isa, then Warsaw and the Advisor, and the three characters together. Would time assist me in achieving that?

I introduced Isa to the Advisor. 'Forgive me, this is our son, Isa. He was sitting alone in his room; I don't know if he can sit with us and keep quiet.'

The Advisor raised his eyes towards Isa. Time froze for a moment, as if it wished to register its presence and overcome space. The weather became cold. I saw a flash of light in their eyes, passing through the whole place. It was the parental instinct that was shared by all creatures. I observed the scene attentively as I was making a comparison between man and the beast. Animals do not lose their way because they do not have a sense of awareness as they follow their instincts, while man strays so often because he owns conscience that overcomes his instinct. I didn't know who was going to win now.

Both stood still, looking at each other. I asked Isa to shake hands with the Advisor, who was speechless. Isa's hand dived into his father's palm, who was mostly silent. Isa pulled his hand and returned to sit beside me. The Advisor moved Isa's chair and let him sit next to him. The Advisor regained his breath and swallowed his saliva to greet him with a few words, 'Hello, sonny Isa.'

Blood flowed strongly in all my veins and my pulse increased. I felt warmth flowing in my whole body and my breath. Did the Advisor know that Isa was his son?

He then added, 'I have just met your father, Sa'ad, and now I will know each of his family. I feel now that we will be friends with the family, not just individuals.'

With his words, I breathed a sigh of relief. I did not yet write these details in Part Two; the events began to write themselves then. The Advisor welcomed Isa and felt his emotion, but he didn't realise he was his own son. Thank heavens! The events of the novel were moving slowly but logically. Warsaw could receive these events willingly instead of getting them all at once, and I could transform the steering of the events into a reality that would perhaps make her happy.

The Advisor overpassed Isa's presence and spoke about his prolific literary product in the novel, criticism and even translation. He talked a lot without receiving real attention from me. My dialogue with him was mere make-believe or pretension, lurking through it the events of the novel which I was writing in contrary to realistic literature.[59]

This scene ended the first encounter between the Advisor and Isa, who only replied "yes" or "no", which urged the Advisor to sympathise with his psychological condition and his sense of estrangement. The Advisor invited us to arrange a family visit to his house in Al Qassim as his guests. I lied, saying, 'But Isa's mother is in Bahrain and committed to her work. I brought Isa with me as he needs to spend more time with me.'[60]

'Bring Isa with you and let him befriend my children; he will find older and younger than him there. There is also my daughter, Sumaya, a child of his age, and he may get acquainted with her and overcome the loneliness he is suffering from.'

A surprise invitation ran in the same timeline which I drew to decipher the puzzles of Part One that Warsaw wrote. But it was another realistic event that would give me clues about Part Two's structure. That would enable my creative task. Events that would write themselves were more substantial than those written by the creative writer. I always admitted to the difficulty of imaginary creative writing. But

---

[59] Dr. Sa'ad, you have always talked about realistic literature. Should the writer categorise his writing between real and fictional? Please, I wish you could finish the novel as soon as possible. I want to be assured of Isa's happiness. Warsaw.

Calm down, dear, but keep your promise. Sa'ad.

[60] Why did you lie, Doctor? This will tire me more and prolong our arrival at the end of the novel. Warsaw.

It is said: the sweetest poetry is a lie. I say: the narrative lie turns real when repeated. Sa'ad.

now I was writing something realistic that tried to break the critical rules set by the antecedents and followed by contemporary critics.

The Advisor left with his eyes fixed on Isa. What was next?[61] Warsaw, you let me now wait for a phone call from the Advisor to invite us to his place and to meet his family. We should both see the results of the events of Part Two, drawing the relationship between Isa and his blood brothers, but strangers to him.

We should wait for the unknown that seemed like death in the novel, causing fear in us because we did not know exactly its essence.

---

61 Doctor, why don't you tell the truth? You are always trying to keep me in doubt, isn't that enough? Warsaw.

    Darling, the pleasure of being alluded by the truth is a constituent of a successful narrative. So, honesty and illusion are narrative necessities. Honesty moves you to the reality, while illusion lets you feel that you are in the centre of facts. That is how I feel now. Sa'ad.

4

A Word Is a True Mirror of the Truth...

The most complicated task was to prepare another part of the novel that dealt with the intended appointment with Isa and his mother, Warsaw. I didn't know exactly how much Warsaw was committed to the narrative structure which I would apply and how much she would assist me in writing and executing till the end of Part Two, or perhaps her motherhood would stand as a barrier to that narrative achievement.[62]

It was an encounter that would reunite the two supposed victims and would be between two main characters in *Victim 69*. That was, between a mother and a child, who was ostensibly an orphan in the presence of his parents. I could affirm until that moment in the narrative that the child did not recognise his mother, but she, indeed, knew her flesh and blood and was prepared to end her life for his happiness.

---

62 I beg you to show full commitment for the implementation of what will be stated in this chapter. Otherwise, the narration will fail to have a humanitarian aspect aiming at the happiness of humans. Sa'ad.

 I promised to grant you my soul and everything I have, Doctor. I only want Isa to have his family right. Please don't be stingy to us with your narration. Warsaw.

Last night I decided to go into seclusion, a sort of hermitage, to write the steps for that part in the draft of the novel and establish the framework for the story.

Nothing was left except the execution. Let us evaluate it after to find out how that literary exercise could have a human dimension, and not an intellectual luxury as many might think. I suggested to Warsaw to meet in what might look like a coincidence in the same café that she used previously to meet the Advisor, due to the private nature of the place for the novel's main characters.

As soon as I told Warsaw of that appointment, she preceded me to the place and took her usual seat; a stereotypical behaviour that would comfort us when we were used to one location. Warsaw thought her psychological state would assist her in getting what she wanted. We entered together, Isa and I, and Warsaw was dumbfounded to see us; everything disappeared in front of her sight. The whole place became dark except for Isa's face, as if she could see nothing except him. She diminished to the smallest size before me. I saw her from that angle, like someone who wanted to pounce and seize the world. Like a lioness, she jumped from her seat towards us, her tears cleared her eyeliner, and her *abaya* fell on the chair; the world darkened before her eyes except for the light of Isa, as if she saw nothing but him. She forgot all that we had agreed on, as if Warsaw wanted to ruin the structure of the novel that I was working on. She was about to hug Isa, but I stood between them. I kept Isa behind me and stood like a solid wall in front of her. I opened my arms to contain her like an eagle and prevent her from doing what she intended to do. Her body stopped, but her soul was about to set free and hold Isa behind me. I had to hold her shoulders and wipe her tears. I took her to her chair; I occupied a seat between them. I became certain then that those people who felt guilty would resign themselves to those who did not feel any guilt. She regarded the tale of Isa as her eternal guilt. In that crucial scene, it was necessary to say that Isa ignored his mother by considering her a strange woman with whom he had nothing in common. I didn't notice any reaction on his part in this situation other than paying attention to the café furniture.

They sat facing each other as she remained silent, gazing at him. She was highly excited and unable to utter a single word. After I had tapped him on the shoulder, Isa began to look at her in amazement and scanned the place in all directions as if looking for something he had misplaced. To break this barrier between them, I said to him, 'This is Professor Warsaw. She is a teacher at the university. She deals with cases related to people, with their problems and their needs. Son, you can tell her if you need anything that upsets you or distresses you in this world and she will help you.'

Warsaw moved nearer to Isa, trying to win him over by asking him if he needed anything. Isa said, looking at me and ignoring Warsaw, 'I want to play with Sumaya, the daughter of Uncle Abdul Rahman. He said he would take me to his home. He said that and still we have not gone there.'

Warsaw asked if Abdul Rahman was the Advisor himself. I answered her affirmatively. She was assured that my narration was in the right direction. I was writing her story and moving its details so that the Advisor admitted his parenthood to Isa, who would later be introduced to his

Victim 69

siblings. Sumaya would be the first. This was precisely what Warsaw wanted in the first part of *Victim 69*.

The meeting lasted a long time; it was full of emotions but was monotonous in its narration. Most of it contained overwhelming motherhood feelings and a child unable to perceive beyond body language and words. I asked her to stay for an hour before ending the encounter. We left the café for our room in the hotel and were followed by Warsaw until we reached the door of the room. She stood, watching us enter one after the other. I looked at her before closing the door and found her kneeling down on the floor like a camel having drained her all-motherhood strength.[63] She remained there, weeping about her ill luck, saying, 'When a person owns something, he forgets it, and when losing it, he clings to it, except grief; it remains in the mother's heart whether it was dead or alive.'

---

[63] Doctor, was I really like that? Or do you just seek suspense only? So far, I have found you moving on a specified timeline, but you have already asked me to write my life events in the first chapter away from adhering to the timeline. Warsaw.

Warsaw, a word can be a picture; it can be a mirror more truthful than the truth. Regarding the narration, we can use both methods, but I will write along with my own vision. From now on, I experiment without adhering or following the trace of any theory which I was committed to; I will break all critical narrative rules. Sa'ad.

5

Talking about Writing is Much Easier than to Write It...

The Advisor received us at his home as he promised during his first meeting with Isa at the Rollins Al Qassim hotel café. I asked Baha to take us from the hotel to the destination address: Villa 43m Rayan Block, Al Qassim. After less than an hour, we reached our destination, passing through paved, clean roads utterly different from the roads of Hijrat Aljabhan. I called the Advisor from the car, informing him about our arrival, and he was more welcoming. We stopped at the villa compound; the guard opened the outer gate, where Baha parked his car. We walked to where the Asian guard pointed towards the main building. The Advisor welcomed us outside the wooden gate. Isa opened his mouth, looking at the swimming pool in the front of the garden. I thought he was comparing the villa with the house where he was living, which looked like a large altar in a giant mosque.

The Advisor warmly welcomed us to his house. From behind the door appeared a beautiful little girl with fallen front teeth. The Advisor introduced her as his daughter, Sumaya. So, this was Sumaya, who was the same age as Isa but a little taller. The Advisor held and kissed her. Then he introduced us to her. 'This is Dr. Sa'ad from Bahrain and his handsome son, Isa.'

I shook hands with the little girl and kissed her too. She also, in turn, shook hands with Isa. He retained his hand in hers; perhaps blood had an electric power that would come into effect by touching hands and, as a result, emotions would emanate. I began to focus on the extent of feelings each showed towards the other; nothing was different. Sumaya offered Isa some sweets, who smiled happily, displaying his features as he was fond of all sorts of sweets. The Advisor took us to his drawing room on the ground floor. His elder son came, and the Advisor introduced him to us too. Then he asked Sumaya to sit with Isa while I went with the Advisor to his office, which was designed with yellow walls and brown furniture. It had vases with plants in all corners. It looked like his office at the university but grander and more elegant. From there, we started the literary dialogue which I intended to conduct there, as I suggested when I called him first. The Advisor spoke about literature as an expert. Then he talked about the novel as overtaking poetry and the dire desire of poets to migrate from the art of rhyming to the temptation of the novel. He claimed that the new novel of the millennium was the anthology of all kinds of literature.[64]

---

[64] I do not want to know these details, and I don't think the average reader will relish them. I just want to know what is going on now between Isa and his sister, Sumaya. Warsaw.

Honey, the events move in parallel scenes. I use the original novel events and the critical events in the text to transform the flow of the story and give it a more realistic picture; it is necessary to make the text logical. Sa'ad.

He referred to many of the prominent Saudi names in the field of letters. He lauded poets, novelists and critics. Then, he mentioned names that he expected to rise through the literary club at Al Qassim University.

After a lengthy and diverse discourse, I suggested that he should pay a visit to the University of Bahrain. It was merely a passing conversation, and I wasn't so sure if it could be fulfilled. He didn't mind but on condition that it should be at an appropriate time.

After more than one hour later, he invited me for dinner in the garden. There, we found Sumaya and Isa in harmony. She was teaching him how to construct different shapes using cubic blocks. I recalled the brotherly relationship between Warsaw and Abdullah at their Uncle Hamdan's house and how it grew more potent when they were away from their father's home. I imagined the connection between Swar and Musa, as if the scene was repeated. Still, in a narration scene, I was optimistic about watching Sumaya pulling Isa by the hand to the dining table. It was a good omen to see them in harmony to that extent. It seemed that brotherly emotions were born unified within us despite adverse causes.

After a beautiful evening, I left to take Isa back to Aljabhan, return to my hotel and then to Bahrain. I wanted to write down all the activities I witnessed over the last few days. It was essential to see Warsaw before I should depart.

The moment I called her, she rushed to the hotel, wanting to know all the visit details that I didn't put down and the description that wasn't part of the narrative structure and I didn't declare. I asked her to take me to one of the highway services station restaurants. There, a man could relax in the desert without hiding anything and merge within the surrounding topographic environment. This was Warsaw's repeated saying, always said whenever she was fed up with the urban life. During the drive, she placed her palm on the fast gear lever. I turned, looking outside, and placed my palm on her hand, pretending it was a natural move. She left her hand without feeling disturbed and said, 'Is there anything in you that looks like the rest of the men? The Advisor, the judge, Butti, Abdullah and many others are alike. You have something like them; all men's sexual desires are the same.'

I pointed out unequivocally that men have similar desires but differ in their ability to control and direct them. She said apologetically, 'The tribal culture opposed that I should be associated with the Advisor; how could I be connected with you and you are entirely different?'

A deep silence fell over us; I didn't know if I wanted to relate to her. I didn't know what made her use that declarative language. The situation made me classify the differences that Warsaw meant as tribal, national and sectarian. What else? Soon I took the lead. 'Warsaw, you are highly educated. You know that a man is not responsible for his differences but accountable for his encounters with the others.'

The tone of her voice changed and began to speak, relying on academic storage; she had a remarkable ability to recall the past. She began explaining what she had said as if I were one of her selected students. She used her academic repertoire like a machine, repeating the same thing. 'We must understand ourselves before understanding the others. Differences are universal rules, while concurrences are human experiences and we are responsible for them. Understanding differences is a human necessity that imposes the need for coexistence and the exchange of interests. We must realise that religion is a sort of worship that establishes the relationship between man and his Lord; that faith is a mode of worship. Religion is concerned with the essentials, while sects are concerned with the divisions and these should not supersede the essentials.'[65]

After this long dialogue – I listened to her with a smile – Warsaw was silent. Her silence was prolonged, and then she changed the tone of her voice. The more I listened to her, the more she became at ease. Women have an awful ability to talk: she began to speak more truthfully. 'These are the theories and hocus-pocus that we teach and, to be honest, we are the first to oppose them. Doctor, we are imprisoned in an iron cell called tradition and customs. To hell with all of them.'

We laughed so much, and her tears flowed down her cheeks and her laughing turned into hysteria. I noticed that women had an awful ability to recall memories and tears alike. They would weep in joy and sadness simultaneously; it was all the same.

I wanted to change the subject. 'Isa was pleased with his sister, which is a good sign of our ability to direct and control the events of the novel, *Victim 69*, the way you want them.'

---

[65] Doctor, don't you think that this method I used in my conversation with you doesn't fit into a narrative language? It looks like it was written and quoted. Warsaw.

I hope we end the second chapter together. I am fragile and broken from the inside; you can be my support. I will do whatever you want to complete the second chapter. We follow the events and will be able to give a happy life to Isa. Warsaw.

After reading this dialogue, I totally agree with you. I would like to rewrite it in a simpler way. I love your highly critical sense, which means a big change in your literary taste. It also shows your ability to change the future of Isa and learn from the mistakes you've made. From henceforth, I can also emphasise that speaking about authorship is easier than authorship itself. Sa'ad

Soon, her state of mind changed, thank God for that. She promised that if Isa returned to his siblings there, she would accept all forthcoming events and be bound to assist me to execute them. I was surprised when she made that generous offer. I asked her to rewrite Part One after taking into consideration the critical remarks that I noted in the footnotes of the text. I said, 'We want the text to satisfy all critics and comply with their theories.'[66]

She reassured me that the moment she completed the part, she would return to it, for she always felt there could be something missing or she did not read. I was fascinated by that charming remark.[67] In return for my request, I had to activate the events of Part Two to make the novel sound realistic, to satisfy me and Isa, and restore his family and social rights.

---

66 Honey, can we really satisfy all critics? Warsaw.

   This question let me laugh, darling. We will never satisfy them all at once. The critic and reader are of two types, either lurking in the text and its writer or cooperating with both. The judgement is implicit and completed before the reading process. Sa'ad.

67 Master, I am now fascinated by the text of *Victim 69*; I am rereading what has been written so far like I've gone crazy. Warsaw.

   On the contrary, darling. The novel that you've read and forgot that you've read it, that's bad. The one you remember the name of, that's normal, but the one you remember its events, that's good, and the one you want to read it over and over, that is an eternal novel. It deserves several readings, despite what critics will find in it, like narrative lapses. Sa'ad.

6

Realism Is to Push a Camel Through the Needle's Eye...

It was evening when Warsaw called, saying she was in the parking lot of Al Qasim Hotel. She wanted me to meet her at the hotel café or the lobby, whichever I wanted. She spoke in a serious tone that I was unfamiliar with, and her request sounded like an order. As I know, a woman does not trust a man who always says "yes", so I declined her offer, in hope she would accept the alternative offer by which I would end Part Two. I spoke about my busy day preparing my travelling bag to return to Bahrain early the following day, and I wanted to finish reading her remarks on the footnotes of Part One. In addition, I wanted to conclude the draft of Part Two. Any delay might disperse my thoughts and lead me to rewrite the two parts. That might alter the plan to reunite Isa and his sister, Sumaya, with their father, the Advisor.

She asked, 'What is your room number?'

I answered in the same room that we spent the night together the first time we met and added that I wouldn't change it as long as I was in Al Qassim until I finished the novel.

Minutes later, Warsaw knocked on the door. She entered hurriedly, taking off her veil. Her black hair spread on her shoulders, and the whiteness of her complexion juxtaposed the black colour of her *abaya*.

I commented, 'What a genuine Arabian filly you are, Warsaw!'

She blushed, feeling proud and tense, showing her anxiety, which became evident in the movement of her hands. She said, 'Sa'ad, don't go to Bahrain, please.'

That was the first time she called me by my first name without any title. She used to call me Doctor, or the critic, or even "my dear". I took that as a good sign of hope. I repeated to her my wish to return home due to prior commitments. She took off her *abaya*, placed it on the armchair, and said, 'You must finish writing the part related to Isa and Sumaya; this relationship is the key to their reunification. I will not let you go before completing it.'

She sat next to me on the couch while my shoulder touched hers. In turn, I moved to the edge of the opposite bed, building a distance between us. She asked for the reason of keeping away from her as she came closer. I went back to the events of the previous part. I explained to her the emotions that overcame me when I felt the heat of Isa's body for the first time. His warmth receded whenever I hugged or kissed him later until it disappeared simultaneously. An electric string spread all over my body, looking for a bosom to receive its flowing current. When I kissed Sumaya, I didn't feel the same emotion. I concluded that I could not finish writing Part Two unless reality existed. She pointed with her hands and eyebrows that she did not get what I was aiming at. I explained that she had more capacity than me to write Part Two because she had the other magnet that would attract the emotions of Isa. Every emotion would be based on an action and reaction. The hunger of the toddler would make the milk of the mother flow. The warmth of the baby would produce the kindness of the mother. Thus, 'You are more able than me to write, Warsaw, because you have the emotions of motherhood.'

If I wrote the part, the "I" would be clear to the reader and I knew that a more powerful text was the one where the presence of the narrating ego (I) disappeared. Then the text would become natural and would convince the receptor or the receiver willingly.

Warsaw understood what I was aiming at; she was the only one with that warmth and motherhood emotions. However, she could not finish the text that I had started. She perceived by her feminine instinct that I had the desire of having sexual intercourse with her so as to have the same feelings towards Isa. She asked, 'Do you want to make love to me like the others?'

'It is a creative need that the writing of the text requires. Love to you will be incomplete without the intercourse.'

She stood steadily, leaving the edge of the bed, stood in front of me and opened her blouse. I lowered my head, covering my face between my two palms, protecting myself from the hurricane of her femininity. She pulled me from the scalp and made me stand before her eyes. Rays from our eyes met, making her speak a discreet language she rarely used. Perhaps language excelled more as the sacredness of the narrative event increased and its temptation overflowed.

'I am ready for you, take me by force, rape me, and with this, write our novel so that Isa enjoys his parents.'

She took me to her bosom, making me squeeze her waist. She swayed, and her lips were wide open. I said to myself, *An experiment would grant the novelist more flexibility and freedom of development and direct the writer to preconceived self-criticism.* In her, I smelled the odour of the men who had passed through her life, those who left their trace saw the phantoms of men and tried to seduce her. They all had gone with the wind. I saw Butti, Saud, A'aedh, the judge and others. I heard the Advisor telling her that phone calls were not the cause of women getting pregnant. I heard that her Uncle Hamdan threatened her after she had refused his firstborn son. I gathered all these men to my heart; I saw them rolling over in her bed, and I completed their mission. I recollected my strength, and then accomplished my task superbly.

I felt the energy of love transferring into the water of life and, with it, I emptied all my memories, thoughts and hope. My mind became vacant to zero; I could give life to any creative text, and I reached the sacred stage that befell the devout in his prayers when his mind was vacant of everything except the praise of God. I said to her secretly as I was accomplishing the mission, 'It is the most genuine manner for creative writing where realism along with it is transformed into a literary genre touching the reader.'

When I completed the task and regained my breath, the filly relaxed next to me to ask me, 'Isn't that forbidden?'

'Not at all. The forbidden relation is the love that the devout call a sin. We are modernists.'

'Has the idea ripened for you now and you could write it down and implement it?'

'Absolutely,' I said. 'For I am captivated by the temptation of writing.'[68]

---

[68] Dr. Sa'ad, I hope this scene is not part of the novel; it's a private narrative for a good cause. Coming back to the narrative structure of which we talk about, and according to the temporal context of events, shouldn't we write the introduction to the second chapter here? So that the recipient can move temporarily with the events. Warsaw.

Prof. Warsaw, this part is just a draft to assist us in ending the novel, and it won't be included at the time of publication. As far as the temporal context is concerned, the traditionalists – as mentioned in Chapter 1– depended on arranging the events according to the time of its occurrence and its gradual development. The modernists, however, look at this arrangement in events and causation and others are simply outworn descriptions where an innovator is not bound to follow its trace during the writing process. This is because innovation generates in the form of one mass and not in the shape of flowing and following particles. Sa'ad.

Part Three

The Omniscient Narrator

Relaxation Is a Cemetery of Creativity...

Since Sumaya was introduced to Isa, she had been fond of him and felt comfortable in his presence.[69] As they matured more, they began to grasp the meaning of life. Since their first encounter at their home on the outskirts of Al Qassim when they were young, Sumaya would call, Sa'ad enquiring about Isa. Sa'ad would normally apologise for being unavailable

---

69 Doctor, by describing Sumaya's feelings, I am certain that the family relationship between Isa and his brothers will be good. You must arrange the events of the novel to the good of Isa and me as well so I can fulfil the dream of my life. Prudent readers will understand that from the beginning. Warsaw.

   Darling, it should be noted that I changed the narrative technique in this chapter. I wish I could disappear, and the omniscient narrator would take my place. He has more capacity than everyone. One of the advantages of an omniscient narrator's technique is that he knows everything about his characters, knows what has come out of them and what is hidden; he is present in the text without appearing. He will help you to know what the characters hide and do; he will let you touch the unseen. In this chapter, we will see Sumaya's feelings like they are universal because the omniscient narrator runs the events of the novel from the beginning to the last. My use of this technique may be a mandate from the characters that I don't deserve because I try to write events according to my wishes, to make the characters driven and negative. You might ask me now if I want to end Chapter 3 after it has overwhelmed me, to let events go as the omniscient narrator decides. But we must wait until the text is turned into a reality. Sa'ad.

due to travelling. She persisted in telling her father about her wish to see Isa when he arrived in Al Qassim with his father. Their calls and meetings were few; however, Isa remained fixed in her memory and it touched her soul.

When Sumaya reached the age of ten, the Advisor decided to enrol her at a foreign school to be proficient in English and learning skills. The Advisor worked hard to take care of his family. He ensured education for his children that befits their social status. He proposed to Sumaya to pursue her education at a foreign school. Sumaya suggested with a child's innocence that Isa should join her. The Advisor was shocked by her request; though he knew about the friendly relationship that his daughter had with Isa, he didn't believe it was that firm. He felt the innocence of this relationship but never knew its secret precisely. He considered innocence human excellence and that he should invest it for the benefits of the two children.

The Advisor called his colleague, Dr. Sa'ad, in Bahrain after the friendly relationship grew stronger between them. He pointed out his wish to have his daughter educated at a private foreign school and asked Dr. Sa'ad about his view of private education. Sa'ad praised this sudden suggestion. Here, the Advisor wanted to take advantage of the conversation and infiltrate the mind of Dr. Sa'ad. He suggested that Isa should be in the same school as this would improve the quality of his education and help him guarantee a brighter future.[70]

---

[70] Darling, I offered you my body and my feelings, so you better appreciate me and carry my feelings to Isa and then the Advisor; don't disappoint me, and don't let me down, please. Warsaw.
I told you beforehand: the writer makes a start but the

After finishing the call, the Advisor wondered about his abundant emotions for Isa, like those for his daughter, Sumaya. Who was that boy who suddenly rushed into their life? And who was that critic who came from Bahrain to Al Qassim on an official visit and in no time the relationship between them turned upside down and became a purely family affair? The same matter concerned the feelings that his daughter bore for that wide-eyed child. He didn't deny his special love for Isa whenever his name was mentioned. There was an ambiguous string pulling him from and to him.

In turn, Sa'ad realised that parental affection was the motive behind the Advisor's feelings towards his son, though he was unaware of that fact; he felt that he should utilise that emotional bond. As for Sumaya and her childish innocence, perhaps God filled her heart with a mass of fraternal feelings, which Isa desperately needed.[71]

The Advisor continued strengthening his ties with Sa'ad and Isa, not hiding his love for that child, whose Bedouin

---

characters themselves end the novel. Until now, I don't know what the Advisor will decide. The omniscient narrator has not disclosed the future yet. I don't know if Isa will stand up to your urgency in the coming events of his relationship with Sumaya. By the way, I miss you. Sa'ad.

71 Sa'ad, your nature prevails your acquired character. Here, you come back to using the reporting language, describing the events rather than narrating them. Here, you hide yourself behind the omniscient narrator. I see you step aside but you still stay in the text! Show me your creation when you rewrite the text before printing. You asked me to live with the reality, and I handed you what I own and what I don't; show me your creativity. Yours, Warsaw.

Oh, filly, who carries an unmatched name: criticism does not find it harmful to have a comprehensive description of places and characters as well as events, but it is also harmless to take your feedback seriously when rewriting events. How does one disappear from the text while you are attached to its writer? Sa'ad.

nature was dominant in his behaviour. He called him "my son" whenever he talked to him to please his daughter.[72]

He invited them to an immediate visit in Al Qassim to brief his friend, Sa'ad, about the designed study plan. One week later, Sa'ad went to Al Qassim. He made a reservation for the same room. He was prepared to bring Isa from Aljabhan. Then he called Um Humood to arrange that.

Sa'ad and Isa met the Advisor and his daughter, Sumaya, two days later. The Advisor embraced Isa and lifted him up to kiss him. He then urged him to shake hands with his daughter. The children went to some chairs by the swimming pool in the front garden, sitting under the shadow of its palm trees.

Sumaya suggested, 'I'll tell my father to give you a mobile phone and a SIM card.'

Isa didn't mind but smiled in agreement, not knowing if he could use a phone at all.

In another situation at the Advisor's office, Abdul Rahman asked his friend, Sa'ad, directly to do something to improve the education of his son, Isa, as he saw how clever he was, which was above the education he was receiving. He told him about the excellent school he planned to send his daughter, Sumaya, to. If Dr. Sa'ad wished for Isa to be her schoolmate, he would always be welcome to do that.[73]

---

72 How much that word touched my heart! Looks like you will succeed in writing a happy ending to the novel, and we will work hard to turn it into a reality. Warsaw.

73 You're such a stingy critic. Don't you know that I'm eager to know what's going on between Isa and Sumaya? Do write down what's going on between them, explain how their relationship grows with each other. Be my darling via your narration. Warsaw.
My beautiful girl, the time of writing or discourse assumes an instant recipient, which is you currently, but the time of the novel assumes

He shook hands with him, assuring him of his financial capacity to do that, and said, 'The bounty is plenty, Abu Isa; don't bother about cash.'

Sa'ad promised him well and told him he needed some time to prepare for the departure of Isa from the country and separation from his mother in Bahrain. He also needed to take the right decision for the benefit of Isa. On leaving the Advisor's home, he called Warsaw. He told her he was at Al Qassim and asked to see her as soon as possible. She was surprised at his being there without telling her. She was optimistic and expected a surprise. She was so happy to see him again. They agreed to meet after her work at the university at Nord Family Café, which they knew very well. He preceded her to the café and chose a secluded corner in the family area, away from intruding eyes and surrounded by trees, and would safeguard the narrative steps of the following events.[74]

Warsaw came within less than an hour. He stood with open arms, welcoming her, and looking in all different directions. Having become assured that nobody was there, he kissed her on both cheeks and praised her perfume. He pulled her by the wrist and made her sit beside him. He said, 'I missed you so much. May I have a kiss?'

'Not here, you fool; people will spot us.'[75]

---

a later reader. The modern reader becomes part of the novel; he is not only a recipient. Therefore, the passing time is limited, while the recipient's or reader's time is open. Let us write the novel for the public, not for its characters. Sa'ad.

74 You didn't mention the name of the family café in the second chapter, but now you specify it by name. Warsaw.

Because now I am the omniscient narrator, I have become the creator of the text and its god as well. Sa'ad.

75 I promise to play the role truly. Trust me, I'll apply what you write entirely. Isa is first and last. Warsaw.

Warsaw was happy to see him again. She didn't hide her longing. She wondered about his sudden arrival and why he didn't tell her earlier about that visit. He explained that necessity had its rules. He tried to explain, but she interrupted him. 'Get to the point.'

Sa'ad spoke briefly about the offer proposed by the Advisor. Warsaw was so perplexed that she became dumbfounded. She hoped well and asked for more details. He put all possibilities on the table in front of her. She removed her head cover, plunged her fingers into her skull and let her hair fall over her shoulders. She was silent and absent-minded. Her features changed from frowning to delight. A smile and some tears were shed, depicting her state of being offended and the feeling of injustice she had suffered as a result. She agreed with strong faith, saying, 'With your help, may this be a good omen?'

Warsaw wished the family relationship between Isa and his brothers be strengthened and that an opportunity would rise to bring justice and normalise the situation. Years passed, and she was waiting for that crucial moment! How hard she worked to fulfil that and found no remedy except by narrating.

Sa'ad obtained what looked like an overall consent from the Advisor, who initiated that proposal and from Warsaw, who delegated Sa'ad to write her novel and worked together to implement it. Also, from Sumaya and what she represented, the innate brotherly instinct. Thus, with these

---

Remember that you're the first text, and you're Derrida who holds the aesthetic value of the text. Any reluctance on your part to turn the text into reality ensures its tragic end; take your caution at every word. Sa'ad.

characters, nothing remained except the adventure of taking that long road that Baha got used to by driving to Rafhaa and then Hijrat Aljabhan.

Baha sat in the driving seat of Warsaw's Corolla, knowing his way to Rafhaa's rest station. Sa'ad sat at the back seat and brought out his laptop and began writing at his ease with his insistence to end the last chapter of the exhausting mission and to relieve Warsaw of her grief and the fatigue of narration. After some tiring hours, Baha stopped at the door of a four-storey building. Sa'ad took his bag while Baha was on his way; he knew where to go while waiting for another phone call from Sa'ad.

Unexpectedly, Sa'ad asked Baha to stop the car and come up with him. The Yemeni receptionist received them. He asked him to have the same room for a night or two. Sa'ad asked Baha to stay in the room until he returned. Sa'ad waited for Abu Humood in the lobby. The man came quickly in his Hilux. Sa'ad sat in the back seat, took out his laptop and started to write.

He reached Um Humood's house. Abu Humood preceded his guest and knocked on the door. Isa was standing by the door. Sa'ad hugged his young one, Isa, raising him to his chest, recalling the same act the Advisor did with Isa. On enquiring about how he felt, Isa asked, 'What have you brought for me?'

He asked him to inform Um Humood about his arrival. Isa returned, accompanied by Um Humood and her sister, Um Rabi'a. After exchanging greetings, they all went into the sitting room. Sa'ad felt uncomfortable of the smell in the *majlis*, and he placed his hand on his nose and asked to have the windows open to get rid of the obnoxious odour. Um

Humood smiled and asked about the unexpected visit. Sa'ad told them that he came to propose the issue of Isa's schooling at a foreign school and that he would take him away from them for some time. That would be a good opportunity to be closer to his mother, Warsaw. The ladies exchanged looks and concealed the expressions of shock. But happiness passed through Um Humood's eyes reluctantly, and she agreed decidedly. However, her sister did not give an explicit approval; she worried about the situation and was dubious about what Sa'ad was saying. Um Humood excused herself for a few minutes. Sa'ad raised his shoulders; he did not have the power to express refusal. Um Humood returned with official papers and an ID card written on it: Isa Sa'ad Ali.[76]

Sa'ad rejected the card, as it showed Isa's photograph and his own name. He was shocked about their knowledge of his real name and how they issued the ID card. He did not reveal his disapproval of their use of his real name. Now, the novel took a turn towards realism; I could now direct its events the way I desire. I own the text, and I am the omniscient narrator.

If Sa'ad failed to show his commitment to what I wanted, perhaps he would lose control of the events. I may kick him out of the novel's events or delegate other characters; indeed, to write the remaining events in the following chapters against his will and far from what he desires. He should remember what the novelists constantly state, that a novelist begins

---

76 I have never asked you about your real name as a kind of respect to your privacy. Warsaw.

Revelation is a realistic narrative. Isa cannot return to your embrace if the narrative is not earnest. The omniscient narrator must have courage to perform; my part here is to be honest, so I don't get disappointed in the situation that I'm involved in. Sa'ad.

writing and that the characters end its events willingly. I feel him swearing at me from his heart, cursing the omniscient narrator and his scandalous narrative technique.

He asked Um Humood and her sister, concealing his surprise, 'Why did you hand me the first card with the name of Humood, while Isa has an official ID? How did you get it, and how did you know my name in the first place?'

As if Um Humood was expecting all these questions. She said, 'We handed you Isa's card when we were sure you were his father and cared for his interests and future.'

Um Rabi'a, in turn, added, 'For how we knew your name was very easy. What matters now is you give us back our son's, Humood's, ID and keep your son, Isa's, card. We issued him a card. Money does wonders.'

Then, surprisingly, Abu Humood spoke. 'Our son, Humood, died one year before the arrival of Isa, and the ID became legible for Isa.'

Sa'ad thanked them for their outstanding care for Isa, and for all the aid given to Isa since his birth. He hoped his future would be more serene and bright.

Um Rabi'a didn't wish this scene to pass peacefully and added, 'We shall provide all Isa's schooling expenses; this is our condition.'

Sa'ad did not grasp all of this and thought that was a kind of madness or raving. Where would they both find all that enormous cash, so that Isa may be admitted to a foreign school and perhaps continue his education abroad? He wanted to explain to them the private and foreign schools that would require high fees, which the residents of Hijrat Aljabhan could not provide.

Um Humood answered clearly and beyond any doubts that, 'Isa has a bank account with more than half a million Riyal deposited, which we think is more than enough.'

Sa'ad paused for a while and began to think. He revised himself but couldn't find what he wanted. He put his hands on his head, squeezing it; he expected to have heard about this amount in one of the parts or chapters of the novel. He patted his forehead lightly and wondered where on earth in the novel he had read about this amount. He excused himself momentarily and opened his laptop, searching in the two parts, One and Two of *Victim 69*. In the search box, he typed, "Half a million Riyals". The answer came quickly. It was the amount that Um Humood demanded from Warsaw (at the time of delivery) in the beginning of Part One. That was in return for delivering services, nursing and then bringing up Isa. Sa'ad gasped, crying, 'What a realistic novel.' As if life repeats itself, and all the writer must do is to choose from its events freely. He had to rewrite them according to his own style.

Sa'ad hit the floor with his fist repentantly. 'Could I not write a realistic novel like this one and be more substantial than that which is based on imagination or imagining?'[77]

He was excited by the intermingling of imagination with reality and its impact on him. There was a thin but strong

---

[77] Doctor, I do not care anymore about your narrative theories, I do not care about them now. We're on the verge of the end of the novel and you're prolonging the use of synonyms? You're tiring and weakening the text and exhausting me. Warsaw.

Dear Warsaw, *Victim 69* was based on realism, then we began to envisage events in which these events became part of imagination. Later, it may become a fantasy novel. Sa'ad.

I'm not interested in theories, but only to bring back Isa, yes, I need my son/Warsaw.

line connecting Um Humood and her sister, Um Rabi'a, to Warsaw. That was what he glimpsed in the narrative horizon.

That was how the events were unfolding and revealing themselves. He asked them about their relationship with Warsaw and why they kept these funds in an account for Isa instead of spending and enjoying its benefits, which was human nature. Um Humood said that they were repaying a debt. 'That was the nature of the Bedouins, being grateful. Warsaw received us in her room when Saddam occupied Kuwait. We shared her room with her, ate and drank, and inhaled the same air, and, and, and…'

Um Humood finished talking, and her sister spoke, 'My name is Jaza'a Khalaf Al Sameri and this is my sister, Harayeb.'

Sa'ad's eyes widened. Now, the events concluded the part he had been working on to end it himself. Events filled him with shocking juxtapositions that would push the reader to run towards future events and would be in charge of the task of suspense. He said to himself, *This is exactly what I state in criticism: the most exciting novel is the one that is already written by its author before he writes its events.*[78]

Jaza'a took advantage of Sa'ad's silence and the solemnity of the situation. She talked about her father, the one that Warsaw designated a space for in Part One. She spoke about her relationship with him since childhood, the relationship between her parents, and the illness that ended his life. She

---

78 Where did you get these events from? Where are you going to take me? I don't understand anything anymore. Are they really my sisters? Warsaw.

   It is the role in which the omniscient narrator assists the writer, to tell what he doesn't know. You didn't know a lot, and here he is, the master; he brings the events back into perspective. Sa'ad.

said it as if reminding Sa'ad about what Warsaw had written not so long. She claimed that her father had twenty-eight children and that most didn't know each other because his three wives came from remote areas like Al Qassim, Rafhaa and Hafre Al Batten.

Jaza'a recalled that time where Hessa asked her daughter, Warsaw, to host them in her room. They didn't know that she was their sister until she asked them to reveal their full names. Warsaw was a child, while Jaza'a and Harayeb were teenagers. They didn't want to disturb the little one by telling her they were her sisters from a different mother. It was the time of war, and the heart would not be open to accommodate them all. They were all living the crisis created by Saddam Hussain. And when fate made Warsaw meet them years later when she came from Al Qassim to Rafha, they knew about their sister. They were afraid that the baby was illegally begotten, so they decided to deprive their sister of her child until his father appeared with truthful evidence.

With the appearance of Sa'ad, they had to repay the debt and value of kinship.[79]

Harayeb spoke, explaining the enigma. She said that Isa had three mothers: Warsaw, who begot him; Jaza'a, who nursed him; and Harayeb, who brought him up. The events started to cast their shadow on Sa'ad himself.

---

[79] I do not want to know these details. I just want to know what is going to happen to Isa. Warsaw.

Darling, it is a flashback or retrieval technique. It depends on the pause of the time of the narrative and bouncing back to the past events. Those events will allow the text to enlighten the reader of what has happened in the past and link the text together. The narrative here has helped you to know your family. You should thank the omniscient narrator. Sa'ad.

He said, addressing himself, *And now Isa has two fathers; Advisor Abdul Rahman, his natural father, but is carrying my name in official documents. It is I who restored to him the narration of life because of my ability to produce a coherent plot. It was I who granted him life, begot him narrative-wise, and from an imaginative novel transformed him into a realistic one. The forthcoming episodes would be irrefutable facts where the father's role would become not mere words but acts and the story would be turned into a cultural state rather than a narrative tale.*

Sa'ad left Hijrat Aljabhan with his son, Isa, carrying official identification documents. He returned, taking with him the events of *Victim 69*. He stopped outside the apartment building in Rafhaa Service Station and asked Isa to stay in the car. He wanted to pay a one-night rent to the Yemeni receptionist for Baha's stay, who would then drive him and Isa to Al Qassim.

Sa'ad went to Room 22 and opened the door slowly, making no noise. He found Baha fully naked, lying on his belly with his mobile phone in front of him. He was sleeping with the photos automatically playing on his phone. Sa'ad picked up the phone to see all the pictures of Warsaw in various poses. The driver, it seems, was masturbating on the pictures.[80]

---

80 Don't write this. You shock me; this idiot can't have been filming me all these years working in my service. You're exaggerating, and you might want to blackmail me later. Warsaw.

It's a realistic novel. The writer sets events according to his personal vision, which loses her credibility. When the truth is shocking, he jumps over it. He is the essential role of the omniscient narrator. We now must recognise his leadership role even if it is traditional; we now must confront the truth. Sa'ad.

Sa'ad took Baha's phone and all his clothes and left him sleeping naked. He left the room slowly, so as not to wake him up. He paid the receptionist the rates for another night. He asked him to tell Baha to wait for him at the service station tomorrow at this time. He left Rafhaa for Al Qassim Rollins Hotel, where the Egyptian receptionist welcomed them.

'Hello, sir, do you need Room 69 again? How many nights this time?'

Sa'ad asked for an unspecified number of nights, as he didn't know when he would finish the novel, what the meeting with Warsaw would lead to, where the instinct of Sumaya would take him, or even how he would deal with the Advisor as he spent more time coming closer to Isa.

In the novel's final part, he decided that it should be on Isa's relationship with his mother, Warsaw. After he finished that part and the whole novel, he would take Isa to his father, whom he still didn't know. Sa'ad spent the night planning the forthcoming events that wove themselves, and all he had to do was to document them himself.

How this novel had exhausted him and how it would exhaust the reader. He wished to get some rest to relax, though this was the cemetery of the creative writer. He, at times, began to grumble at his agreement with Warsaw's offer at the end of Part One.

He made a phone call to Warsaw, telling her about Isa being with him. He proposed to meet her as they did the last time. They agreed to meet at 12pm the next day. He arrived at the appointed place ten minutes earlier, as he wanted to keep the description of the place fixed in his memory. However, Warsaw foiled his plans by arriving at the same place one hour earlier. She received him with mixed feelings the moment she saw him coming. Emotions overflowing from his narrative text and others from real life. She dropped her veil and drew him to her bosom, hugging the fate that was writing her novel. He said, using the same sentence of her in a previous scene, 'Warsaw. Not here; his is a public place and people can see.'

Her desire for him was not sexual or even personal. She was yearning to smell the smell of Isa through him to regain her foresight and calm her fears. Masculine desire rose in him while she touched its source. He took her to a corner far from evil looks. He felt her, embracing her waist and suckling her lips; he nearly swallowed them.

She scolded him with fondness, 'Sa'ad, shame on you! I see that you like this thing.'

He said he was blowing into her the wind of Isa, and that pleasure does not bring happiness, but the result of happiness was the joy of the language of her novel. He retreated to his chair and looked around him. Nobody was near them, and they thanked God for that and the dominant customs a little. She asked him about Isa and what had become of his schooling. She wanted to know about the life he would spend with his sister, Sumaya, and his father, the Advisor.

Sa'ad said, 'Harayeb and Jaza'a agreed to the issue of his schooling.'

Warsaw denounced the agreement of Harayeb and Jaza'a regarding Isa's future. She referred to what she mentioned earlier: that they were merely a midwife and a wet nurse and that she had paid them half a million Riyals for services rendered. She accused me then of lying and betraying reality. Sa'ad didn't want to confirm the discovered relationship between her and her sisters.

He sufficed with what she wrote in the text so far. 'I preferred to keep suspense present till the end of the novel, because it will keep your eyes focused fully.' He reminded her of some of what she wrote in the past: the novelist should not write everything; he must retain something for the reader. This is the style of modern fiction, the cultural novel where there is a major role for the reader. Because he provides some ends to the events and leaves the rest to the reader to share with the writer in his creative text. It is not possible to acquire a creative reader if we do not prepare a solid foundation that pushes him to the text.

He said this explicitly, 'You must be patient when reading a text; it must take you by surprise and then pull you in to play a role. I hope that what you do is for the benefit of Isa.'

Warsaw was afraid that I would leave her with Sa'ad in an open ending without any decision taken about the fate of a mother. She implored him to take into consideration her tragedy and that of her son, Isa, and never stop writing the novel until the text is satiated as he was satiated from her earlier. He wanted to explore the situation; he recalled that whenever he returned to the text, he desired her immensely. That relationship that left the author constantly wishing to connect with the text.

He said to her, 'I desire you whenever I want to complete the text; you better pay allegiance to the critic whenever he excels in his work.'

She agreed to his proposal, which would never end and wished for a happy ending to this novel that was not realistic anymore. He assured her that it was a novel that might take a few years to plan an end for and that she must be at his disposal, according to the agreement. He must work at ease while concluding events as she wanted. He promised her to stay in touch with Isa as he built his academic and familial future, even if for years.

She agreed, and he said, 'It is the post-modern role of criticism where the critic treads on the text and the characters respectively.'

***

After a literary and time leap into the future, the final chapter of Part Three is devoted to Isa and Sumaya.[81] Studying together abroad added to their harmony, making them feel the relationship that bonds them. A natural love energy flared up in them. Isa wanted to transfer that energy into a natural human behaviour graced by a lawful marriage. He sought to lure Sumaya whenever there was an opportunity; she reciprocated and declared her love to him. Thus, from time to time, he would sneak some kisses. He found in her his beloved partner and wished her to be his wife. She was recalcitrant and coy, making her more desirous. He saw in her his lost half, and she found in him a partner of life who would realise her dream of motherhood and share with her the vicissitudes of life. Both relied on that stout relationship built by the Advisor and Dr. Sa'ad. Isa suggested the announcement of their engagement be in a European style; that is to say, as his friend and not a fiancée. He proposed

---

81 I do not think I can see the future. Your text has become unseen, and I have been walking with him at his will. Warsaw.

In this type of time jump, narrative time is present, while natural time is non-existent. In the last section of the novel, we talk about its feed and conclusion, in which narrative time can be less or more than natural time. Sa'ad.

to her for the first time in the presence of his colleagues in school by kneeling on his right knee while his left leg was upright. The audience looked at them, as he presented a gold engagement ring to her.

He kissed her finger, then her hand, and kissed her in front of them all, who applauded them happily and wished them a blessed life ever after.

Isa and Sumaya lived a natural life full of love and waited for the right moment to inform the Advisor first, who would undoubtedly bless their step. She suggested that Isa tell her father first, as his agreement was guaranteed.

This would save him the effort of opening the issue of their engagement with his father, Dr. Sa'ad. Isa called the Advisor when Sumaya was sitting beside him, caressing the locks of his hair falling on his forehead like a coy virgin. He greeted them and then stuttered as his forehead involuntarily sweated. The Advisor knew that there was something about Sumaya. He asked him, 'Uncle Abdul Rahman, would you allow me to propose to your daughter, Sumaya, after our graduation ceremony next month?'

The Advisor didn't think long, as if a hidden matter was pushing him to accept it. He informed Sumaya's mother, who gave him a free hand to decide. He called his friend, Dr. Sa'ad, and told him about the issue without any introduction. Sa'ad kept quiet for a long time, listening to the devilish proposal. The Advisor felt that there was something of a mystery in the matter. He asked his friend what made him so hesitant, and Sa'ad told him, 'Dr., it is the will of God and yours; you command and Isa will oblige. However, give me some time to consult his mother first.'

Sa'ad went back to the last draft of the novel; he had to write the end himself and create the right solutions that would please both Warsaw and Isa. But he left me, the omniscient narrator, a free hand because there remained one section that he couldn't write. I removed some events from his control and took hold of them willingly as an omniscient narrator.

Sa'ad called Isa in attempt to dissuade him from his wish to marry Sumaya, but he was determined and resolved on his desire. I reminded Sa'ad of Warsaw's stubbornness and determination inherited from her mother, Hessa. Then, he knew that nobody could dissuade him. So was Warsaw and her mother, Hessa, before her. Ask the radio if you don't remember. There was no need to waste time and energy after all. Now, he could go again to Al Qassim to talk to Jaza'a and Harayeb after they had agreed to sponsor Isa's education. He would be returning to the first cycle! What could he do? How could he deal with forthcoming events?

He called Harayeb and Jaza'a to tell them about an urgent matter. They were surprised and afraid that something wrong had happened to Isa. They received him outside the house, with age taking a turn on them. Abu Humood had grown older and so did Harayeb, and Jaza'a put on more weight, and her knees could not bear the extra kilos.

Sa'ad stood outside the house, refusing to go in, avoiding adding another part to the novel. Without any introduction, he said, 'The Advisor wants your son, Isa, to marry his daughter, Sumaya, who is studying with him: what do you think?'

Harayeb was happy to hear the good news, while Jaza'a was hesitant as usual, wanting to know all details before making any decision. She used to hear much about the Advisor and his status through the calls Isa made to them; Harayeb agreed, but Jaza'a made a condition to meet Warsaw before deciding. Warsaw wished to meet her sisters. Sa'ad was dubious about this condition. Their meeting may divert events from the proposed plot of the novel. This may add another irony that would please the critics but would add a burden to Sa'ad, who eagerly wanted to put an end to the novel. Sa'ad promised the ladies well and asked them to give him time to arrange a meeting for the mother-sisters.

Sa'ad returned to Al Qassim cursing Baha, the driver, whenever he passed the station, recalling his past events. He asked to meet Warsaw; it was the decisive moment in the novel. How could he tell her about the destiny that conflicts with man's nature and his destiny, even if he were a critic or an inspired novelist? It was an awful failure; could he accept it? He wanted to evaluate himself. He had to investigate his negative experiences, not the positive ones. He asked to meet her at the same time as their last meeting and in the same venue. Being unaware, she cancelled her lectures, for the sake of the narrative, and asked her two children, Musa and Sewar, to accompany her before the appointed time. Warsaw wanted Isa to get acquainted with his half-brother and sister before I wrote down "finished", declaring the novel's end. I couldn't care less if some described me as the "damned narrator".

Sa'ad was nervous and saw Musa and Swar in the prime of their youth. Warsaw introduced them to him. He welcomed them but stuttered unconsciously. How could he bring the subject of Isa's marriage to her? He excused himself to being alone with their mother, Warsaw.

'Professor, Isa wants to get married.'

She was optimistic and thanked God for that. She also congratulated Sa'ad for his succeeding plans and for finishing her novel. She thanked him for his help and appreciated helping others in the name of literature. Through these services, the critic becomes worthwhile in this life.

He interrupted her. 'Isa wants to marry Sumaya, the daughter of the Advisor, who has already agreed.'

Warsaw could not control herself due to this horrid surprise. She felt a pang in her heart. The movement of her hands became difficult. The effect gradually moved to the rest of the body. She fell to the ground and passed out. Sa'ad shouted at the top of his voice. Her two children and the hotel employer gathered around her, followed by the hotel staff. One of them called for an ambulance, which arrived in no time to take her to Al Rass General Hospital in Al Qassim. She remained at the Emergency Unit for one night. The next day she was conscious at noon, but had a hysterical fit. She was given a sedation in preparation for a complete check-up.

Before the arrival of Warsaw's brothers and her mother, Sa'ad left the hospital for the café where the incident took place. He asked for her travelling handbag. On opening it, he found a file written on it: *Victim 69, Part Two*.

At the hospital, Warsaw's condition deteriorated. Swar called her uncles, Abdulla and Mohammed, asking them to hurry up. An hour later, they came with their mother. They went to see the physician, who told them that Warsaw had a severe psychological shock resulting in a nervous spasm causing hemiplegia and loss of speech and movement. She would remain in the hospital for a long time. Swar asked the physician about the possibility of her improvement, who replied with the usual automatic answer, 'Everything lies in the hands of God.'

Two days later, before leaving for Bahrain, Sa'ad wanted to pay a farewell visit to Warsaw. He went to see her in her private room at the hospital. He entered her room to see her under the mercy of illness and the white linin. He could only see her opening eyes. She tried to speak, but her tongue failed her. Hot, dried tears dropped on her cheeks. Approaching her, he sat at the edge of her bed and said, 'Warsaw, or as your grandfather called you Derrida *bint* Derrida, now you represent the most beautiful linguistic text. Now, you have become a critical topic to which I could apply the deconstruction theory of Jacque Derrida and others.'

Sa'ad came closer, whispering into her right ear, introducing her to what Jacques Derrida said in respect to Deconstruction Theory: 'It is not mere opposite and negative deconstruction of the text but a duplicate reading. There, the text passes through readings; a traditional reading that fixes its explicit meanings. This is what I was good at in Part One, and a deconstruction reading which opposes the first text. This is what Sa'ad completed in Part Two.' He whispered in her ear, 'Thank you, Warsaw; thank you, the most beautiful Derrida.'

The next evening, Sa'ad called the Advisor on his return to Bahrain to tell him, 'We delegate you to accomplish the wedding of Sumaya to Isa. His mother fell sick. I shall stay with her and visit you at the earliest time possible.'

Sa'ad returned to Bahrain, feeling proud of himself after completing the comments on Part One, writing Part Two, and assigning Part Three to me, the omniscient narrator.

Victim 69 lies within his hands now. He cannot see any role for anybody except his own efforts. He ignored me just as he did Warsaw, as if he had been infected by megalomania. He now owns a novel criticising a society and finding it irresistible to any criticism. He aimed at distancing it from any embellishment but to write about reality and deconstruct its features no matter of the consequences.

He stood on Shaikh Isa Causeway, breathing the sea air, recalling what Warsaw had been doing with every problem facing her. He removed the SIM card from his phone, threw it into the sea, replaced his contact number with another, protecting himself from the worries of writing and the problems of critics and criticism. He breathed a sigh of relief. Now he could study Warsaw's literary output without worrying, because it was usually possible to study the production of some writers after their death, as they had accomplished their creative experience. With death, the writer's authority or influence on critics disappears, as there would be no intellectual censorship of creativity. With her hemiplegia, Warsaw's authority had disappeared, and the reader is born after the death of the author. Thus, after the novel's publication, Sa'ad should see the amount of clamour it causes. Then, Sa'ad should honour Warsaw for her creativity in writing Part One because a tribute to creative writers usually is observed after their death.

Accomplished.